World on a Maple Leaf

A TREASURY OF CANADIAN MULTICULTURAL FOLKTALES

An Initiative of United Cultures of Canada Association

Edited by Asma Sayed and Nayanika Kumar

 Human Rights
Education and
Multiculturalism
Fund

 COMMUNITY
SERVICES

World on a Maple Leaf: A Treasury of Canadian Multicultural Folktales is an initiative of United Cultures of Canada Association (UCCA), with financial assistance provided by the Human Rights Education and Multiculturalism Fund and the City of Edmonton, Community Services.

UCCA, the publishers and the editors are not responsible for copyright or any other related issues.

The stories in this collection express the thoughts of their authors. They are based on their personal experiences, or the transmission of the stories to them from their friends and families, or their own research.

ISBN 978-1-55378-134-9

Printed in Canada

Contents

Acknowledgements

On behalf of United Cultures of Canada Association, I am very pleased to present this collection of multicultural folktales to you.

We all are proud to be living in a country that not only practises, but also promotes and celebrates multiculturalism as an official government policy. This book presents our multicultural heritage in a nutshell. Each story in this collection is unique in its grace, wit, humour, wisdom, philosophy and purity of spirit. All together they make this collection deeply engrossing and breathtakingly beautiful, almost mesmerizing. So is our heritage.

This project would not have been possible without the gracious support of the Human Rights Education and Multiculturalism Fund and the City of Edmonton, Community Services. A special thank you is due to Nicholas Ameyaw, Senior Consultant, Community Engagement and Inclusion (CEI), Alberta Culture and Community Spirit, for his valuable insights and guidance in developing this project.

We were truly fortunate to have the guidance of Catherine Ripley, Carol Suddards and Asma Sayed, who brought to this project their several years of experience and unique expertise in the area of children's literature. We remain indebted to you all for the hundreds of hours of your precious time that you spent discussing, analyzing and critiquing these stories. Without you, this book would not have been what it is.

Thank you, all the authors for your contribution—you have gathered veritable gems for this collection. Thank you, all the reviewers. Your comments were critical to the development of this collection.

Thank you, Dana Antayá-Moore, for taking it on for publication. You and your team have embellished our work with master strokes of perfection. Thank you, Flavio Rojas, for the wonderful illustrations. Thank you, Helen Adhikari and Karen Haukedal, for designing and copy editing this book.

And now, a special thank you to the Board and staff of UCCA—Grace Megli-Turner, Lisa Riou, Katherine Davies, Latika Srivastava and Nayanika Kumar. Thank you, Latika Srivastava, for your legal research on copyright laws as they apply to folktales. A special thank you is due to you, Nayanika Kumar, for creating this project. You dreamt a beautiful dream and translated it into this beautiful book.

The first 1000 copies of this collection will be distributed free of cost to places where they can be made available to many children, including children's hospitals, emergency shelters, community organizations and other such agencies. Proceeds from the sale of other copies will go to the UCCA's Children's Fund, that supports children who are in critical need by providing small grants to them.

We hope you all will enjoy reading this book as much as we all have enjoyed working to create it.

Christine Beaver
President
United Cultures of Canada Association

Introduction

ON CANADIAN MULTICULTURAL FOLKTALES
BY ASMA SAYED

World on a Maple Leaf: A Treasury of Canadian Multicultural Folktales rejoices in the multi-culturalism of Canadian society; multiculturalism is the identity of Canada, and makes Canada a distinctive nation on the global platform. The Multiculturalism Act, legislated in 1988, has given Canada a unique standing in the world, as a nation promoting and celebrating plurality. In a multicultural society, people from diverse cultures not only live together, but also love to do so. They not only tolerate the differences of cultures and languages, but appreciate, respect, and enjoy them. The multiculturalism policy of Canada identifies that multiculturalism is a fundamental part of our heritage and national identity. In multicultural Canada, we are free to follow, share and advance our cultural heritage and language. The policy encourages everyone to appreciate and endorse diverse cultures and practices. It invites everyone to participate in the development of all aspects of Canadian society. It also directs all Canadian institutions to be respectful of Canada's multicultural character.

Canada is a microcosm of the world; there are people from more than 200 different cultural backgrounds living in Canada. As people migrate to Canada, so do their tales. People from around the world bring a wealth of experiences, stories, recipes and languages, and further enhance the multicultural make-up of the country. As people embrace Canada and its values of freedom and equality, their stories and experiences become part of the Canadian landscape. The stories in this collection are written by people from different cultural backgrounds who have called Canada 'home.' Thus, we call these stories Canadian multicultural folktales. While some of the stories have originated outside Canada and then travelled here with people coming from other parts of the world, others are distinctly rooted in the Canadian soil. Stories such as "The Soup Bone" are a testament to the pioneers who worked hard, sacrificed much and built communities. Pietro, the protagonist of the story, toils relentlessly and saves to bring his wife to Canada; but, in the meantime, the soup bone that he had given up benefited many more people and thus helped establish a community. This soup bone holds the symbolic value of the sacrifices that have been made for building the Canadian nation. We believe that such stories need to become part of Canadian children's understanding of the nation.

And yet, there is a lack of children's literature that celebrates the distinctiveness and richness of the cultural wealth that various communities have brought to this nation's vibrancy. Canada has a rich history of children's literature including works such as Catherine Parr Trail's *Canadian Crusoe: A Tale of the Rice Lake Plains,* Ernest Thompson Seton's *Wild Animals I Have Known,* L.M. Montgomery's very popular *Anne of Green Gables,* and many more works offering various pioneer stories, and stories of wilderness, nature and animals. Canada's children's literature is splendid, and offers multi-faceted entertainment and 'edutainment,' and there have also been several volumes focusing on particular cultural experiences. There have also been many interesting collections of stories presented by First Nations authors—Ella Elizabeth Clark's *Indian Legends of Canada,* Christie Harris's *Once Upon a Totem,* Frances Fraser's *The Bear Who Stole the Chinook,* and Basil Johnston's *Tales the Elders Told: Ojibway Legends,* are some examples. But there is a dearth of children's collections focusing on the multicultural nature of the country.

The collection presented here is rendered differently in its gathering of works by authors from varied backgrounds, including racial, cultural, religious and ethnic; the authors are united in their attempts to speak to Canadian children. Including works from various immigrant communities that have settled in Canada, as well as from the First Nations whose cultures and traditions are rooted in Canadian soil, this anthology seeks to identify the diversity of Canadian society. We have asked the authors to re-imagine the stories they heard from their parents, grandparents, friends and families, and to write them for Canadian children, who will benefit from the treasure of oral tradition that people have carried with them and brought to Canada.

A folktale, which is our focus here and originates in oral tradition, is "a short narrative in prose of unknown authorship which has been transmitted orally; many of the tales eventually achieve written form" (M.H. Abrams, *A Glossary of Literary Terms,* p. 124). Folktales, which include fables, anecdotes and legends, are a core element of any culture and are the foundation of many literary traditions. The authors of the stories in this collection heard the stories either as they were growing up or as they traveled around the world. Oral tradition is ever changing, and as such there are no 'original' versions of the stories in this collection. Readers may have read some of these stories in different versions, and thus may find them familiar. The stories may also be recognizable as, at times, similar stories exist in different cultures. It is interesting to note parallels in folklore from around the world. For example, this collection includes a story titled, "The Girl Who Married the Morning Star," from Blackfoot culture. There is a comparable story from *Panchtantra* titled "The Girl Who Married a Snake." The Indian story has likely been influential in the Western tradition; for example, it may have had some bearing on the story of Cupid and Psyche.

An interest in these kinds of stories helped encourage the birth of this collection. We started this project by sending out a call to various communities and cultural groups. We got an overwhelming response; the stories were also reviewed by the community members and their feedback was incorporated into the overall selection process. It was not only difficult to choose stories, but at

times also painful to reject them, as majority of the stories that were received were fascinating. In sorting out the stories we have tried to ensure that they are representative of the various cultures that exist within the Canadian mosaic; thus an attempt has been made to not repeat stories from a single culture unless there were compelling reasons to do so. For example, Anansi is a very strong cultural symbol in West African culture, and is found in many stories. We have thus included two stories here that have Anansi as the central character; both the stories are gripping. "Anansi and the Turtle" is humorous and gives the messages of cleanliness, hospitality and sharing to children; "Anansi and the Sky-God" is rooted in the mythology of the African culture. We have chosen "Anansi and the Sky-God" as the first story in the collection as it explains the existence of stories in human life within a mythical framework. On the other hand, the last story of the collection, "The Storyteller," urges us to carry on the tradition of storytelling and pass on our stories. It is our hope that our readers will become chickadees, like the one in the story, and continue to tell and read these stories to their next generations, and thus will keep on adding to the multicultural fabric of the country.

Thus, the purpose of the book is to entertain and educate children, and to help them understand the intricacies of growing up in a multicultural nation. The tales carry a glossary to explain culture-specific terms and, wherever necessary, contextual information is provided to enable a better understanding of the stories. However, it should be noted that, historically, folktales have always been modified and retold. With every retelling, a folktale is recreated and reinterpreted; thus these tales are always open to interpretation. While the original culture of the stories has been identified, we are aware that the folktales do not 'belong' to any particular culture; our attempt is simply to recognize how stories travel and change as they migrate.

As much as the stories originate in different cultures, there is no attempt here to claim that this collection is 'complete'; if anything, it is representative of some of the cultures that have become part of the broader Canadian cultural framework. Canada's history comes together at the crossroads of Aboriginal, English, French and other immigrant communities. As such, this collection brings stories from a variety of backgrounds; but, practically, it is not possible to include stories from all the cultures in a single anthology. This anthology simply serves as the beginning of what we hope will be a series of new collections.

While today's children and childhood have been struck by what Jack Zipes, a leading children's literature scholar, calls the 'Disney Spell,' the stories presented here are a breath of fresh air. Today's children are either too engrossed in Disney films or in playing games on their TV screens or computers. Technology and its advances have brought wonders to contemporary society, but have also endangered the traditions of storytelling and communal sharing. This collection is an attempt to reclaim lost traditions, and to remind our society of the richness that stories can bring to our children. Rooted in cultures from around the world, the stories not only offer a different imaginative world to the children, but also provide an opportunity to learn different languages, albeit only a few words of each, as they delve into the world of spiders and foxes, kings and farmers, old women and young maidens, from China, Japan, India, Ireland, Afghanistan, Lithuania and around the world. These stories will give children an opportunity to study various cultures that have become part of the wider Canadian culture, and see that, as Canadians, they have a lot in common with the children from different backgrounds, and that there are universal elements that we all share as humans, irrespective of national, religious, ethnic or racial differences. Some of the stories teach children the importance of honesty, hard work and sharing, and the values of human rights and equality. For example, "The Fig and the Whistle" gives a light-hearted glimpse into French folk tradition, and yet teaches resilience and respect for elders. There are stories that are distinctly Canadian; for example, both "The Soup Bone" and "The Cape Breton Giant" are stories that early settlers shared, and they let children learn chapters of essential Canadian history.

How do we get Canadian children to come together and see the similarities in the differences? This question is often raised. Storytelling is a medium by which children can understand each other and the world around them in simple terms, and yet take important steps in learning. Readers, especially children, can read the stories in this anthology alongside some other more popular tales, and interpret them in their own way. While there certainly are some universal elements to the stories, each reader will find a different meaning; comparing various tales will give readers an opportunity to indulge in an entertaining and exciting experience. These stories, put together, promote the universal ideals of sharing, honesty, perseverance, truth, helping the needy, and defeating evil. The children reading them will recognize this universality, and comprehend the distinctive representation of the essence and spirit of the culture; the stories will open their minds to positive qualities of other cultures, and persuade them to respect differences. Feelings of appreciation will replace the distrust, ignorance, biases, fear and hatred that create rifts on the grounds of racial, religious and cultural differences. As the author of "The Storyteller" notes, "Sometimes, in Canada, we ask about a person's statistics or facts, but we forget to ask about a person's journey. But by sharing stories, we learn not only how much we have in common, but how much we depend upon each other, as a community." As such, the key message that the stories presented here deliver is that of unity in diversity. As the farmer tells his sons in the story "The Farmer and His Sons," "united we stand, and divided we fall." Standing together and looking at difference as precious helps remove fear and distrust. We hope that the stories can be a valuable learning tool for school children, as well as ESL learners, and that this collection will be useful at various levels and will add to the existing repertoire of children's literature in Canada.

Anansi and the Sky God

A TALE FROM WEST AFRICA

BY PHYLLIS WALKER

Long, long ago in West Africa, there lived a special spider with magical powers, great skills and awesome intelligence. His name was Anansi. His special job was to bring rain to stop fires, and to perform other jobs for his father, the great Sky God—Nyame. Anansi seemed to be happy. But, in fact, he was very unhappy and just pretended that life was good. Every night, before he fell asleep, he thought about his secret sorrow. Anansi wanted to own all of the stories in the world, but he knew that the stories belonged to his father, the great Sky God Nyame, and that he would not share them with anyone.

Anansi's dream soon became a goal and he began to plan and put his mind to this one dream. To want something means that one has to plan and work to achieve the goal—whether to become a better baseball player, to play the drums or to become the best speller that one can be.

So every day, Anansi spent time planning and deciding how he would approach the Sky God. He studied many new stories and practised every day. Each evening, just before the sun began to set, he went to a clearing in the forest, and in front of some of the animals, he told a story that he had studied. Anansi wanted to be ready in case the Sky God asked him to tell a story when he visited him. Each evening, he asked the animals to vote and tell him which story was their favourite. He kept practising until he was very good at telling stories and he was ready to put the second part of his plan into motion.

One very hot day, Anansi spun a magic, strong, silky cord and threw it up, up, up to the blue sky where Nyame, the great Sky God, lived. Then he climbed up, up, up the cord to the home of Nyame. Rolling up his silken cord, he tucked it into his pocket and followed the winding road to the court of the great Nyame. At the gate of the court he asked to see the great Sky God. He was let in and escorted by the soldiers until he stood in front of Nyame. Anansi bowed the low bow that he had practised, as Nyame looked down at him from his great height and spoke, "Tell me, oh my son, what is it that has brought you here to my court?"

"Oh Father, O Great Sky God Nyame," responded Anansi, "it is my dearest wish to own all of your stories so that I might take them out from here and share them with the world. To share will bring great happiness to your heart and to the hearts of many others. Why should all the stories remain here in the sky when the people on Earth could enjoy hearing them? If you would let me have them, I would collect those stories that are here, locked in a box, and take them out to all the people on Earth."

Nyame looked down at the tiny, tiny spider and told him that his stories were not for sale and so Anansi should go away, back down to Earth. Anansi was so unhappy that he had failed, that he returned to Earth: but, he began to make a new plan to win over the great Sky God. Three times he failed, but he never gave up. On his third visit to Nyame, the great Sky God gave in and told Anansi that he would let him have all the stories if Anansi brought him certain things.

"Bring to me," said Nyame, "Onini, the powerful python, Osebo, the lively leopard, Mmoboro, the mighty hornet and Mmoatia, the fanciful forest fairy. If you bring me all these things, I will give you my stories to share with the world." So Anansi bowed low and took his magic cord from his pocket and slid back down to Earth.

Early the next day, Anansi went off into the forest, deep into the bamboo grove, and cut down the tallest bamboo pole that he could find. He went with it to the place where Onini, the powerful python, lived. Anansi put the bamboo pole near the home of Onini and began to pretend that he was talking to his own wife, Aso Yaa.

"No, you are wrong, Onini is longer than this pole," said Anansi. "No, you are wrong, this pole is longer than Onini," said Anansi, in a pretend voice so that he sounded like his wife, Aso Yaa.

This make-believe conversation continued for a while until Onini poked his head out of his home and asked, "What is all this talk about me and a bamboo pole?"

"Oh, Brother Onini," said Anansi, "it is I arguing with my wife, who insists that this pole is longer than you are, and I tell her no, you are longer than this bamboo pole."

"Well, we can solve that easily," said Onini, "I will stretch out beside the bamboo pole and you can measure me and see for yourselves. Where is your wife?"

"She is too shy to come out from behind the palm tree, but I can do the measuring now," said Anansi. And with that, Onini stretched himself out beside the bamboo pole and Anansi ran around trying to measure him, without much success. Finally he told the snake the problem was that, because he was shaped like the letter 'S,' Anansi could not get a good measurement unless he tied him to the bamboo pole. Onini agreed to this and Anansi gathered some vine creeper to use as rope, to tie Onini securely to the pole. Once he had succeeded, Anansi began to skip around the snake and shout, "Now I will take you to the great Sky God—Nyame!" Using his magic powers, Anansi transported Onini to the clearing behind his hut and went off to gather the other things.

Searching through the trees, Anansi came to a huge hornets' nest. He climbed the tree that the nest hung from, and went to a branch above the branch holding the nest. Anansi perched in the tree and began to sprinkle water onto the hornets' nest from the gourd he carried.

"Oh, Brother Mmoboro," called Anansi, "it is going to rain. You don't want to get your beautiful wings wet. Come into my gourd and take shelter."

"Thank you, Brother Anansi," said the hornet. He flew into the gourd and Anansi put the lid on, sealed him up, and climbed down from the tree. Laughing, dancing, and singing all the way to his house, Anansi was full of joy as he thought about how close he was to succeeding with his goal to get all the stories from Sky God.

Anansi had an idea about how to capture Osebo, the lively leopard. He took down his magic stick and commanded it to dig a big hole and prepare a cage. Once the hole was dug, Anansi inspected it. The hole was as wide as the leopard was wide, and three times as deep as the leopard was tall. Anansi knew that once the leopard fell into the hole he would not be able to escape. Covered all over with branches and leaves, the hole was hidden from all the animals and when the leopard came walking by that night, he fell down into the hole and awakened the entire village with his roars. He could not escape from the hole and there he remained until the next day.

Early that morning, Anansi came to the hole and peered in. "Oh, Brother Osebo, what are you doing in that hole? Have you been drinking that palm wine?" asked Anansi.

"Anansi, please help me out of this hole," said Osebo.

"Oh no, I am scared of you and maybe you will harm me when you get out," said Anansi. Osebo promised that he would not harm Anansi and so Anansi lowered two sticks for the leopard to climb onto to get out of the hole. While he was climbing up, Anansi put the cage over the hole and into it went the leopard. One quick magic spell meant that Osebo was sealed in the cage and transported to the back of the house. Anansi held his magic stick high in the air and waved it over Osebo. Osebo sank slowly to the floor of the cage and fell fast asleep.

Anansi felt triumphant; he had everything except the forest fairy, Mmoatia, and he knew just what to do to capture her. So, off he went to prepare for her. He carved an Akua doll and took it to the tree where the fairy came to play each evening. He filled the doll's hands with mashed plantain and hid behind a tree. As the first rays of the setting sun touched the odum tree, the beautiful, iridescent wings of the forest fairy beat quickly in the evening breeze as she came to investigate the doll with the delicious food in her hands. The fairy tried to pull the bowl away from her, but could not, because Anansi had glued the bowl to the doll's hands. He had also covered the bowl with glue so that the forest fairy stuck to the bowl. Mmoatia then kicked at the doll and both her feet got stuck to the doll. There was no escape. Anansi came out, laughing, from behind the tree.

"Ah-ha!" exclaimed Anansi. "Finally I have gotten all four things that Nyame wants and I will take you all up to the Sky God." Anansi went off to the witch magician and asked for a special spell to enable him to take all four things up to the home of the great Sky God.

Immediately after that, Anansi, Osebo, Mmoatia, Onini and Mmoboro arrived at the gates of the home of Nyame. The guards let them in, and once he arrived at the Great Hall, Anansi bowed low in front of the great Sky God and presented him with the four gifts. Nyame was amazed and called all his men to him. They stood and stared in amazement at all that the tiny spider had accomplished. Nyame led his men in singing songs of praise to the tiny spider, Anansi. "Aiyee! Aiyee! Aiyee! Anansi, you have proven yourself. Please free Osebo, Mmoatia, Onini and Mmoboro, so that they may go back to their homes."

Anansi freed all four. Nyame then said, "From this day on, all the stories will belong to Anansi so that he can share them with the world." Nyame raised his mighty brown arms above his head, placed one hand on top of the other and blew the stories into Anansi's mind, never to be forgotten.

"Now tell us all a story, Anansi!" said Nyame. As he stood up in front of the Sky God Nyame and told a wonderful story, Anansi was happy that he had practised and practised for many evenings in front of an audience. To the sound of loud applause, Anansi climbed down the long silky cord to share the stories with all the people on Earth.

Author's Note

Anansi is a mythical spider figure from West Africa, and the stories about Anansi mostly belong to the Ashanti culture. The Ashanti people have kept alive many ancient traditions and much culture, with Nyame as their supreme being. The slaves who were transported from Africa to other parts of the world found hope in the stories of Anansi and kept the stories of the tiny spider alive by passing them down from generation to generation. Because the Ashanti people lacked a written language at that time, the stories survived in oral tradition and were handed down by special tellers who were called *griots*.

The Akua doll in the story is a fertility doll commonly found in Ashanti homes and given to female members of the Ashanti people.

In this story, Anansi demonstrates the importance of having a goal in spite of obstacles and of being prepared for opportunities when they are given. Anansi perseveres and gets all the stories, which are then passed on to the people on Earth.

The Soup Bone

A Canadian Folktale
by Melissa Morelli Lacroix

Back when settlers from around the world came to Saskatchewan to farm the land, there was a man named Pietro, who lived alone in a little shack on a prairie homestead. Like many of the men around him, Pietro lived a simple and frugal life in an attempt to save money to send back to his sweetheart in his home country, so she could sail to Canada to join him. Whenever Pietro made any money from his crops or his services, he quickly dropped it into an old sock that he hid in a hole, dug in the dirt floor underneath his bed. From time to time, he took out the sock and counted the money accumulated there. Then, with a sigh and a wish, he put the sock back into its hole and continued saving.

Finally, after many months of working and skimping and saving, the day came when Pietro's sock was filled with enough money to send for his beloved Lucia. He stuffed the sock safely into his pocket, then hitched his horse to his sleigh, and rode over the snow-covered prairie into town, where he promptly went to the bank and handed his sock full of money to the teller. "Please," he said, "I would like to send this money back home, so my sweetheart can join me here in Canada."

"Certainly, sir," the teller replied, as he pulled out the necessary forms and papers and began to stamp and scribble. "She should have the money by the end of the week."

Pietro smiled and nodded with pleasure. "Thank you!" he shouted in gratitude as he squeezed the teller's hand. "Thank you! I shall bring my Lucia to meet you as soon as she arrives!"

"Please do," the teller replied.

Pietro smiled widely as he left the bank and walked down the street to the post office, where he posted a letter to his sweetheart, announcing the good news. Then, still smiling as if he were a boy at Christmas, Pietro made his way to the butcher shop, where he pointed to the largest, meatiest soup bone in the shop and declared, "That one there! By George, today I will celebrate!" And soon, after an exchange of money and pleasantries with the butcher, Pietro stepped back outside into the cold winter air, with the soup bone wrapped in brown paper. His heart was soaring so, and his mind was so distracted by the events of the day, and thoughts of the warm savoury soup he would prepare upon his arrival home, that he almost ran right into his friend, Luigi. "Oh!" Pietro exclaimed. "What luck to meet you! I have such good news—I have sent for Lucia to join me."

"That's good," Luigi responded weakly, forcing a smile.

Pietro noticed his friend's weak response and became concerned, "Why, Luigi, what's wrong?" he asked.

"My wife is sick," he said sadly, "and the children also, and we haven't anything more than a few shriveled potatoes to eat. What shall I do?"

Without a thought for his own supper, Pietro pushed his brown-papered soup bone into his friend's hands. "Take this," he said, "and add the potatoes to make a good soup. Your wife and your children will soon get better."

Luigi clasped the package in his hands. "Thank you, friend," he said, and tears filled his eyes as he spoke. "May your kindness be returned to you."

The men embraced and bid each other good-bye. Pietro's stomach grumbled as he headed home, but instead of thinking of the big, meaty soup bone he would not have, he thought of his sweetheart Lucia and the journey she had ahead: the winding trek down from their mountain village, the rollicking steamship passage across the Atlantic, the jerky cross-country travel aboard a drafty train. Pietro remembered the journey well. It had been tiring and difficult, but exciting, too. He hoped his Lucia would fare well.

The weeks passed, and Pietro continued his frugal habits so he could save for the imminent arrival of his beloved. He skimped on the kerosene and firewood he used to heat his home, and he ate simple, simple meals: bread for breakfast, potatoes for lunch, boiled water for supper. He did not have much, but what he did have, Pietro wanted to save for Lucia.

Finally, after snowstorms and blizzards, the day came when Pietro's sweetheart arrived. Pietro rode to town with his horse and sleigh and met her at the station. After a long embrace, Pietro hoisted Lucia's trunk and luggage up onto his sleigh and took her by the arm. "Come, my sweet," he said, "I want you to meet someone before we go home." He led her down the street and through the town to the bank where he found the teller who had helped him send money to Lucia.

"Ah, Pietro," the man said, smiling, when the couple stepped before his wicket. "I heard your sweetheart was arriving today. Please wait here." The teller rushed away, but soon returned with a small pail. "I have something for you and your wife."

"Oh, how kind," Pietro replied. "What is it?"

"A welcome gift for Lucia," the teller replied. "It's from the whole community."

Pietro raised his eyebrows with pleasure and surprise. "Really?"

"Yes," the teller nodded. "You know how hard this winter has been. So many people have been sharing and helping one another." Pietro nodded; he knew well the hardships of the winter, for he had both given and received help from the other settlers of the village—a push out of the snow, a cup of flour, a chicken egg.

"The other day," the bank teller continued, "a man came in for some help with one of his loans. He had no money to make a payment, but he had a soup bone, a little bit boiled already, he confessed, but still meaty and tasty, he assured me. I accepted the soup bone and did what I could for him.

"I took the bone home and told the story to my wife. She was shocked by the idea of paying a debt with a used soup bone, but she took it and boiled it with some potatoes and onions. It was a most delicious meal.

" 'I've heard of this soup bone,' my wife said, as we ate. 'The man who gave it to you got it from the priest who took pity on the poor state he was in.'

" 'That was kind,' I said, 'but this soup bone is so meaty and flavourful I can't believe that it has already been in two other pots.'

" 'Two,' my wife laughed. 'Oh no! This soup bone has been in more pots than that, many more pots indeed. The priest,' she explained, 'got the soup bone from the Clavelles for performing the baptism of their new baby. The Clavelles got it from the doctor's wife when the baby came. The doctor got it from Yasmine Shariff when he tended to her broken foot. Yasmine got it from Oi Lam for knitting him a pair of socks. Lam got it from Annia Lekka, when he helped her husband repair the roof after one of those blizzards. Annia got it from Margherita Pedrotti for tending to her when she was sick. Margherita's husband Luigi got it from someone, but no one seems to know who—someone doing errands in town one day, they say. Whoever it was, he was just coming out from the butcher's shop with a fresh meaty soup bone under his arm, when he saw Luigi all worried about his sick wife and children. The man handed the soup bone over to Luigi without delay, and the rest, well, I've just told you.' "

"That is quite a tale," Pietro said, shaking his head with a chuckle for the story of his soup bone.

The teller nodded. "Indeed, but it is not yet finished. Now it is your turn." The teller presented his pail to Pietro. "Please take this soup bone as a sign of welcome to your sweetheart. May it feed you both well and make Lucia feel welcome."

"I am sure it will," Pietro smiled as he reached for the pail. "I am sure it will."

AUTHOR'S NOTE

The Soup Bone is a based on a true story that happened to my great-grandfather, Pietro Morelli, in the early 1900s in rural Saskatchewan. It is a story that I heard as a girl at family gatherings and read in my community history book. My family always laughed at the humour of the story, but was also proud of its message of community spirit and pioneer sharing.

The Amethyst Flower

A Polish Tale

BY MARIA TERESA OLSZEWSKA HOPKINS

Come, all, and listen to me, because I wish that Gotfryd's deed be known to all and for ages to come!

Long ago, in the Polish court of King Zygmunt II August, the knights passed their leisure time bragging and boasting about the glorious deeds that they did to prove their courage to the ladies of their hearts. The king was greatly entertained by his knights' theatrical performances. On one of those days, they were drinking the famous Polish mead, *Miód Pitny,* and each knight, in turn, tried to impress the company with his fantastic idea.

First, Arthur *Zapalczywy* boasted, "For the most beautiful lady Blanka, whose eyes radiate like the stars, I would fight seven knights at once."

Then Jan, the young, well-mannered knight, named *'Piękny'* for his pleasant looks replied, "That would be too small a deed for my lady Jolanda, with a voice like silver bells. I would honour my lady by sailing a fishing boat through the Bay of Sea Monsters. Eh, what am I saying? I'll swim the bay!"

Only Gotfryd was quiet. The king listened with a kind smile. "And what about you, Gotfryd?" he asked. "What deed would you dare for my daughter Roksana?"

"I'm thinking, Your Highness," replied Gotfryd, "but unless I go in search of the enchanted *amethyst* flower, any deed would be too small to be worthy of this golden-haired lady of mine!"

"What is this enchanted flower?" asked the king, "I have never heard of it."

"How is that possible?" asked Gotfryd. "The flower grows within the boundary of your kingdom on the high mountain called *Niedostępna.* It was planted by the Mountain Fairy King, who surrounded it with a ring of fire and put his daughter, Wiwiana, there to guard it. Only the truly brave—one who can step into the ring of fire fearlessly—can pluck the enchanted *amethyst* flower. If a man has the slightest apprehension, the flames will burn him to ashes."

"I have heard of this flower," said an old *burgrave.* "It has golden stamens, petals of the transparency and hues of *amethyst,* and leaves that shine with all the colours of the rainbow. This flower has magic powers; the one who possesses it will not only understand the tongues of flowers, trees and birds, but it will also bring back health to the sick, and make the ugly beautiful and the old young again. Truly this deed would honour our princess."

Arnold of Trevil, whom Gotfryd had defeated in the past, was listening with anger. After a few goblets of mead, he laughed, saying to Gotfryd, "It's easier to brag over wine than to carry out one's promise!"

But the king, seeing Gotfryd go pale, said, "Unwise are your words, Count Arnold. Everybody knows that Gotfryd *Zwycięzca* is fearless and steadfast, even if he exaggerates a bit. We know that Gotfryd said this to show his reverence and love for Roksana. Anyway, the other knights did the same by bragging about their deeds, boasting as always."

Arnold of Trevil, taking a sip of golden mead, replied, "I know well this game of boasting, but even in boasting there must be a limit. Otherwise he could say, I'll pull out the tallest pine from the castle garden and bend it at one end into a hook, then put one mountain on top of the other and climb up to get the moon from the sky and offer it to the princess, so she can wear it as a medallion on a golden chain!"

All the knights and even the king couldn't refrain themselves from laughter. But Gotfryd, who was not accustomed to being mocked, burst out in anger, saying, "You are mistaken, Count Arnold, by taking my words as futile talk. You're mistaken! Know that I'm leaving right now on my quest for the enchanted *amethyst* flower to bring for the princess, and if I do not die, I shall surely bring Roksana the flower!"

The king began to worry, seeing that this was not a joke anymore. "You act unwisely, Gotfryd, to make such a serious statement. It is a different matter to stand in defence of the oppressed, but for a boast it is futile to risk your life!"

Perhaps Gotfryd would have calmed down and resigned from the promised quest, because at heart he knew that the king was right, but at that moment, Arnold spoke again.

"Your Highness, let him go to that mountain, and make sure he takes a pine log so he may at the same time bring down the moon!"

Now, none of the king's persuasions worked; Gotfryd was determined to go. He said, "I swear by my knight's word, that today I leave the castle for my quest, and if I do not die, I'll bring the *amethyst* flower for the princess!"

After that, no one could oppose him, since a knight's word is a matter of honour. One who broke it would become an object of ridicule and disdain. Before Gotfryd parted company with the princess and the knights, the king said, "Know that I have thought for some time to give you my daughter for a wife and make you successor to my throne. When you come back with the *amethyst* flower, you shall have her hand in marriage."

Cheered up by this, Gotfryd replied, "Your Highness! Even if not just one, but a hundred fire rings I need to pass, I'll come back happy, knowing that I win such a prize!"

Hastily, Gotfryd went on his quest, and soon came to the foot of the mountain *Niedostępna*. Bravely and cheerfully he climbed it, thinking of his future, and then he stepped into the ring of fire. The flames parted, and Gotfryd saw the enchanted *amethyst* flower. In silent admiration he looked at it for a while, then stretched out his hand to pluck it. But then someone touched his shoulder and he turned around; behind him stood a charming lady with eyes of *amethyst* and rainbow wings.

"Gotfryd!" she said, "I beseech you, do not touch this flower! It is the flower of my life, and my father surrounded it with the ring of fire for my protection. If you pluck it, I shall die."

"Beautiful lady!" replied Gotfryd, "Rest assured that I'll not touch this flower. I'll leave, and neither the king nor the princess Roksana will blame me for coming back empty-handed when they hear what I have heard from you."

"I am sorry, noble knight," said the mountain princess, "but if you tell why you did not bring the flower I'll also be in peril of my life. If it were known that a knight passed through the flames unharmed and also listened to my plea for mercy, Merlina, the Queen of all fairies, would punish me all the same. Your sacrifice must be kept secret."

"How can I?" shouted Gotfryd. "I am the knight whom they call the unvanquished one! I would ridicule myself, telling them that I broke my promise! I would become a laughingstock. Don't you understand, Wiwiana, that I cannot do this?"

"I see that's true," replied Wiwiana quietly. "You cannot do this. No, no, I have no right to demand such a sacrifice! Then pluck the flower which you have earned; I see that I must die!"

But Gotfryd stood quiet and motionless, doing some hard thinking. "No, Wiwiana!" he said finally, "I'll not pluck this flower! It would be a despicable action, unworthy of a righteous knight!"

"If you don't do it, everyone will call you an ignoble person and ridicule you."

"Yes," whispered the knight, "but to avoid being called coward, shall I become a criminal? For vain boasting, shall I sacrifice your life? No! Truly I cannot do it!"

"What about Roksana?" asked the mountain princess.

"Roksana," repeated Gotfryd. "She will turn away from me with disdain, and she will hold me in contempt."

"You see, I am right, Gotfryd. Do not hesitate any more, or I myself will pluck it for you." She reached for the miraculous flower, but Gotfryd stopped her hand, saying, "I will not be happy, Wiwiana, knowing that my happiness was gained by such deed. Good bye, Wiwiana."

"Good bye, Gottfryd," said the fairy, seeing that he had made up his mind. "I'll never forget that you saved my life. Take with you this ring and remember that you have, in me, a friend and sister." He thanked Wiwiana for the gift and set out on the journey home.

When the guards at King Zygmunt's Wawel Castle spotted Gotfryd approaching on his horse, they passed the news to the king and the princess. The king called all the knights to the great throne hall and said to them, "Soon our noble knight, Gotfryd *Zwycięzca,* will arrive, and it is my wish that he be greeted with respect. He is bringing the enchanted *amethyst* flower, which he earned by passing through the ring of fire, and for this he will get the prize of the hand of my daughter."

"Do we know for sure that Gotfryd earned the *amethyst* flower? Perhaps he is coming empty-handed," murmured Arnold of Trevil. Even though he didn't dare to say it out loud, it was heard by the closest-standing knights, and they reprimanded him.

"Anger and jealousy are blinding you, Arnold, to make you say such things! You know well that no one of us would go for this flower. If one goes bound by the knight's word, he would rather die than come back empty-handed. How dare you accuse Gotfryd *Zwycięzca* of such cowardice?"

Arnold felt ashamed and lapsed into silence. At that very moment, the pages opened the door to the great hall and Gotfryd walked in. He stopped in front of the king and Princess Roksana. He didn't dare lift his face to her, but the princess stood there with a bright smile. She was heartily glad to see him again and wanted to hear how he had prospered in everything. "Welcome Gotfryd, my steadfast and fearless knight," the king said. "I see that there is no force that you would not defeat. Give to my daughter the gift that you acquired, and you, Roksana, give him your engagement ring."

While the king spoke, Gotfryd stood sadly, not looking at anybody. The king wondered what this could mean, so he asked, "Aren't you content with the reward you're about to receive, or is there no enchanted flower growing on the mountain *Niedostępna?*"

Gotfryd replied, "Better than anything in life would be the prize of the hand of Roksana, and the flower is still growing on the mountain *Niedostępna.* But I didn't acquire the flower, my king, so I have no right to receive the ring from Princess Roksana."

Astonished even more, the king asked, "What happened, Gotfryd, that you come empty-handed?"

Gotfryd lowered his head to his chest, and hesitantly, as if the words he was about to say couldn't pass his throat, he said in a quiet voice, "Your Majesty, when I saw the big ring of fire around the enchanted flower, I was shaken with fear, realizing how daring my promise was, so I took fright of terrible death, and left with nothing."

All the knights listened in astonishment, wondering if they had heard it correctly or if it was really Gotfryd *Zwycięzca* who had said these shameful words, so unworthy of a knight. If anybody else had said it, they would have laughed, given him spindle and distaff, and expelled him from the knights' circle. But Gotfryd's fame made everybody take it with silence and astonishment. They were so touched, as if the shame had fallen on them too. Even Arnold of Trevil was silent.

Just then, the melodious voice of the king's daughter was heard: "Truly, I do not believe it, Gotfryd!" Shaken by the words of the princess, all the knights looked at her standing beside the throne of her father. Trembling, Gotfryd looked at her now for the first time since he had entered the great hall after his quest. He looked into her face; she continued, "I don't know why you came back without the *amethyst* flower, but I know that it was not cowardice that made you come back empty-handed! I do not insist upon explanation because I see that you cannot reveal this. I love you and trust you, and my ring belongs to you!"

Gotfryd stepped forward and knelt at her feet, crying like a child. Then Roksana said to the collected crowd, "Of little hearts are those who at first judgement of a friend believe that judgement, even though it came from his own mouth! Gotfryd, aren't these your friends with whom you have gone through many dangers? How can it be that you are the bravest of them all, and yet they can believe without hesitation in your dishonour?"

Shameful feelings came over the knights at their own behaviour. How could they suspect Gotfryd of cowardice? Who among them would not tremble for a moment while stepping into the flames? Surely there must be some secret to it, so that he could not act in his own defence? Shouldn't they trust him without asking to know the reason for the failure of his quest? Only then did they start coming closer and, one by one, start to shake his hand in reassurance of their friendship.

Suddenly, a strange rainbow light appeared in the big hall, and the astounded knights turned toward it. They saw a golden-haired lady with eyes the hue of an *amethyst,* with rainbow wings at her shoulders and the enchanted flower in her hand.

"I didn't want you to suffer any longer, Gotfryd," said the fairy lady, looking at Gotfryd and Roksana. "I came here to clarify your noble deed for all to hear. But I see that it is needless to add a fairy's testimony to one who possesses the trust and loving affection of Roksana. Listen to me all: King Zygmunt, Princess Roksana, and you, noble knights! Gotfryd had to pass the hardest trial of strength, which is to defeat not an enemy, but his own pride and vanity. So, take this flower, Gotfryd, which you truly earned. Truly you are a righteous, noble knight." Gotfryd took the enchanted *amethyst* flower from the hand of the fairy and gave it to Roksana.

Author's Note

This tale is set in the context of courtly life during the reign (1545–1572) of King Sigismund Augustus (in Polish: Król Zygmunt II August). The court was held in the old Polish capital city of Kraków, where on Wawel Hill the palace of the Polish kings still stands. King Zygmunt August was the last in the line of the Jagiellon dynasty which reigned in Poland for two centuries. He did not have a male child to whom he could pass on his reign, which greatly troubled the king, who spent his leisure time surrounded by the young knights who came to his court from all over Europe. The story set in the time of King Zygmunt places it clearly in the Polish Golden Age, when Polish culture flourished and the Polish kingdom reached its greatest expanse.

The Amethyst Flower, which I first read as a teenager in the collection *Nasza Księgarnia* in the year 1963, is part of a longer historical story by Halina Górska entitled, *O Księciu Gotfrydzie Rycerzu Gwiazdy Wigilijnej* (About Gotfryd, Knight of the Christmas Star) and was first published in 1930. Our teacher recommended honesty, defending and protecting the weak in our society, and keeping our promises. The story also reminds us of the principles of friendship. The importance of the story in Polish culture lies in showing exemplary behaviour for young people, and in praising the noble character of young men—righteous, unfaltering and courageous— and of those who keep their promises. I was impressed with this tale when reading it as a young teenager. In my adaptation, this story not only borrows the material, but uses the style of the educational story, which I feel strongly obliged to pass on to others, for the value of its message is timeless.

Glossary

amethyst—a violet gemstone that, as a form of quartz, is found in crystalline clusters sometimes called the 'flower of life'

burgrave—the hereditary lord of a town and its surroundings

miód pitny—mead (literally, 'drinking honey')

niedostępna—inaccessible

piękny—beautiful, handsome

zapalczywy—quick-tempered

zwycięzca—vanquisher, conqueror

The Cape Breton Giant

A Canadian Legend
by Ed Butts

No other legend is more loved by the Cape Bretoners than that of Angus McAskill, the Cape Breton Giant, who was not only big and incredibly strong, but also had a big heart to match. He was born in 1825 on the Isle of Harris, Scotland. While he was still small, his family moved to Cape Breton Island with other Scottish pioneers. They settled on a farm near the village of St. Anns. Angus was an average-sized boy, and the other members of his family were all people of ordinary stature.

But when Angus was not yet 14 years old, he began to grow at a much faster rate than the other youth his age. And he kept growing! By the time he became a young man, he was an amazing seven feet, nine inches tall and weighed 450 pounds. He had broad, powerful shoulders, muscular arms, and a muscular chest. His father had to raise the ceiling in their house so that he could stand straight, and his mother had to make giant-sized clothes for him and order an extra-large bed. His Scottish neighbours called him *Gille Mor,* Gaelic for 'Big Boy.'

Angus was always pleased to use his great strength to help his family and neighbours with the hard work of a pioneer farming community. At barn-raising bees, he could single-handedly carry beams that several grown men couldn't budge. He carried heavy barrels of flour, one under each arm, as easily as if they were toys. When it was his turn to gather firewood, he would carry the load on his back because he found the ox too slow. In order to help the fishermen, he would turn a fishing boat upside down to drain the water out of it, and then set it upright again so that the fishermen did not have to bail it out with a bucket.

One day, when Angus and his father were plowing the field, a neighbour bet them 10 dollars that they could not finish the job by sunset. His father took the bet, but before they could finish the plowing their horse went lame. Angus did not want his father to lose the bet. So, he unharnessed the horse, stepped into the harness himself, and began pulling the plow. The news spread like wildfire; people gathered to watch and began to shout that *Gille Mor* was as strong as the horse he had replaced!

Hearing all this, Angus's mother came down from the house and saw her son labouring like a horse. Even though the crowd was cheering him on and singing his praises, she was not amused. She was worried that Angus might injure himself in all this, so she pleaded with him to stop. Angus could have easily finished plowing and won the bet. But he could not refuse his mother. He took off the harness as his mother had wished, and paid the neighbour 10 dollars.

At sunset each day, Angus would go down to the shore to help fishermen haul their boats in. One day when he went down to the wharf, he saw a sad-looking man sitting by a boat that was tied to the dock. The man was a poor farmer whose crop had failed and he now had no food for his wife and children. He had come to the docks looking for work and asked the captain of the ship if there was something for him to do. The captain told him that if he could unload the barrels of flour that were in the ship's hold, he could take one of them home. Then he walked away, laughing at his cleverness. There was no way the poor farmer could even move the barrels.

Hearing this, Angus went down into the hold of the ship. Moments later, a barrel came flying up through the hatchway and landed on the dock. It was followed by another, and another, until the hold was empty. When the captain returned, he was astonished to see all the barrels piled up on the dock of the ship. The poor farmer he had laughed at was sitting on one of them, with a big grin on his face.

On another occasion, Angus's neighbour had fallen very ill and urgently needed to see a doctor. The nearest doctor was at least 40 kilometres away and a terrible blizzard was raging. The roads were so clogged with snow that the horses could not get through. Angus took the sick man on his back, and carried him the whole way without once setting him down.

Stories about the Big Boy and his incredible strength began to spread all over Cape Breton. A man, who had the reputation of professional fighter, challenged Angus to a fight. He thought that beating Angus would gain him great fame. But the gentle Cape Breton giant did not like fighting. He knew that with the power in his arms he could seriously injure, or even kill, a man. He did not accept this challenge.

When he was 20, he was approached by a circus promoter who had travelled to St. Anns to meet this farm boy with the strength of Hercules. The promoter asked him to join the circus. Angus had never been far from home. He was very reluctant to leave his family and friends, but he accepted the offer as it gave him an opportunity to earn a lot of money for his family.

The promoter billed Angus as, 'The Cape Breton Giant.' He was a sensation wherever he went. People gasped in wonder as he picked up a water barrel that weighed over 100 pounds, and took a drink from it as though it were nothing more than a tea cup. In another popular show, he would walk out in front of the circus audience carrying his performing partner—who was only three feet tall and went by the name of Colonel Tom Thumb—in the pocket of his big coat. Before the audience, he would take his partner out and place him on the palm of his outstretched hand. His partner would dance a jig on his palm and then put up his fists and pretend to challenge Angus to a fight.

As a circus strongman, Angus travelled all over Canada and the United States. He also toured the West Indies, and visited England where Queen Victoria declared him the biggest man she had ever seen.

The most famous story about the Cape Breton Giant is also the saddest. One day, when he was in New York City, Angus decided to go down to the harbour for a stroll along the docks. Smelling the sea air always reminded him of home. Colonel Tom Thumb went along with him for company. Of course, all of the people at the docks stared at the Giant and his tiny companion. A group of sailors asked Angus for a demonstration of his strength. One of them pointed to a big ship's anchor that was lying on the dock. He dared Angus to try to lift it. The anchor was made of solid iron, and weighed more than 900 kilograms. Angus had never lifted such an enormous weight before. Tom Thumb did not like the idea. He warned Angus not to try it. He told the sailors that if they wanted to see a demonstration of the Giant's strength, they could buy tickets to the circus.

The
CAPE BRETON
GIANT

But the sailors kept coaxing Angus to show them what he could do. He looked at the anchor, and wondered if he could lift such a heavy object. He had never tested his strength to its limit. This was the chance, so Angus said he would do it. When Tom Thumb tried to talk him out of it, Angus assured him that everything would be okay. Angus took off his coat, and then studied the anchor. It had a long shaft, and at one end there were two hook-shaped flukes. He positioned himself at the part of the shaft that was nearest to the flukes because that was where the weight would be concentrated. Angus knew that if he were to lift the anchor successfully, balance would be of the utmost importance. Angus squatted beside the anchor and grasped the cold iron in his big hands. Then, using a method that weight lifters call the 'press lift,' Angus hoisted the huge anchor. With a roar and a mighty surge of strength, he stood up straight and triumphantly hoisted the massive anchor above his head. The sailors looked on in wide-eyed disbelief. Had they not seen it with their own eyes, they would not have believed that any human being could have performed such a feat. Tom Thumb looked on with growing anxiety. He just knew in his bones that something bad was going to happen.

Standing there with the anchor raised above him, Angus felt the thrill of victory. He had done it! But even he could not carry that monstrous weight for long. Now he had to put it down, and that was easier said than done. If he just tried to slowly lower the anchor down to the dock, it would become unbalanced, and the sheer weight would cause it to drop and crush him. Angus decided that his only option was to toss the anchor away from him. This might have worked, but he chose the wrong direction. As Angus threw the anchor, and the mass of iron fell, one of the big flukes caught him in the shoulder. The irresistible force dragged the Giant down. Tom Thumb's worst fear had come true. The cheers of the sailors turned to cries of dismay. The accident with the anchor probably would have killed any other man, but Angus was still alive, his shoulder badly injured. His days as a circus strongman were finished.

Over the years, Angus had saved up a considerable amount of money. When he returned to St. Anns, he used the money to set himself up in business as the owner of a general store. He became widely known for his fair and honest dealings.

Angus McAskill died quietly in his sleep at the age of 38, from what was then called 'brain fever.' His grave overlooking St. Anns Bay can still be seen today. Under his name on the gravestone are the words, "A dutiful son, a kind brother, just in all his dealings, universally respected by all his acquaintance. Mark the perfect man and behold the upright, for the end of that man is peace." In a little museum near the grave you can still see Angus McAskill's coat and bed. A life-sized portrait of him gives visitors an idea of just how big he was. And all over Cape Breton Island, people still tell stories about the Cape Breton Giant.

AUTHOR'S NOTE

This story, which is a mixture of fact and lore, is part of the Scottish heritage of Cape Breton Island, Nova Scotia. The events take place in the mid-nineteenth century. The central character, Angus McAskill, embodies such virtues as humility, responsibility, respect for others—particularly parents— and the understanding that the strong should help others, not take advantage of them. The Giant McAskill tales are important in overall folk culture because they are based on a real person, not a fictional character, and they illustrate how ordinary people will make a folk hero out of a man who was larger-than-life not only physically, but also in his good will toward others. If there is a moral, perhaps it is that of the danger of pride, as shown in the story about Angus and the anchor. As a son and grandson of Cape Bretoners, I have been familiar with the stories of Giant McAskill since I was a child.

Masha and the Swan-Geese

A Folktale from Russia
by Nataliya Bukhanova
and David Schultz

Once upon a time, a little girl named Masha lived with her mother, her father and her baby brother, in a small house, at the edge of a small clearing, at the edge of a small village, at the edge of a great dark forest.

Masha tried to be a good girl. She obeyed her father, and helped her mother with many of the chores. She enjoyed helping her mother, and liked it when her mother spent time with her. Ever since her little brother had arrived, however, it seemed to Masha that all that she ever did was chores. All her mother ever seemed to do was take care of her little brother, and she never did anything with Masha anymore.

One day, her parents called Masha, and announced that they were going away to the city. Masha was excited to think that she would be going on such an adventure, but they told her that she would not be going.

"*Nhyet, Mashenkia,* you must stay and look after your brother," her mother said, cuddling the little boy in her lap. "He is too small to make such a long trip—he's only just learned to walk."

Soon the day came. *"Milaya Dochka,"* her mother said, kneeling to speak to Masha. "Do your chores, and be a good girl."

Masha nodded slowly, but looked wistfully over her mother's shoulder at the cart ready to take her parents off to the city.

"Most importantly, Masha," her mother continued, tying her scarf over her head, "do not leave our yard, and watch over your brother. If you don't, Babba Yagga's *Gusi-lebedi* will come and carry him off."

Masha promised she would take care of her brother and would not let Babba Yagga's Swan-Geese near him. Her mother hugged Masha, then she hugged and kissed Masha's little brother, and soon the cart was rolling down the road and away, while Masha waved goodbye. She waved until her arm hurt, so she waved goodbye with her other arm. Her brother had stopped waving long before that. As the cart disappeared, Masha turned and saw him happily playing in the dirt at the edge of the garden.

Masha realized that, for the first time in a long time, she had no chores to do. Beyond the fence of their yard, the flowers of the clearing smelled sweet, and the green grass was the perfect height for running through. Without a second thought for her little brother, Masha climbed over the fence to run and play.

She was having such fun that she did not see the sky darken, nor did she hear the strange sound coming from somewhere in the sky. Only when she felt a strange breeze did she look up and see them—seven great birds, which looked like swans, but with the drab brown feathers of geese—the *Gusi-lebedi,* the Swan-Geese. They were honking and hissing as they flew over Masha, and straight on toward her house. Only then did Masha remember her brother. She ran to try to get to him, but on their long wings, the Swan-Geese swooped down well before Masha reached the fence.

The nasty birds gathered around the little boy, honking and hissing among themselves. Then, taking hold of the little boy's clothes in their beaks, and with three great beats of their wings, lifted him up into the sky. Flying back the way they had come, over Masha, then out over the great dark forest, they carried Masha's little brother away, and were soon lost from sight.

Masha stood, shocked and silent. Then her chin began to quiver, and from her eyes, the tears began to flow. With a wail of protest and despair, she began to run, following the Swan-Geese. Masha did not know where the Swan-Geese had gone; she only knew that she had to find her brother. She ran and she cried. She cried and she ran.

The forest became dark and strange, until Masha, who was becoming a little afraid, came to a small clearing. In the centre, there stood a great apple tree, its branches heavy with ripe fruit.

"Hello, little human," said the tree, speaking slowly, its voice a mix of the whisper of leaves and the groan of branches in the wind.

"Sister-Tree," said Masha, her voice hoarse with her tears, "please tell me where the *Gusi-lebedi* flew. They have taken my little brother and I must find him."

"Oh, my dear little human," replied the tree, "I think that they flew this way, but my branches are so filled with apples that I am afraid they might break. Please climb up and pick some and I will be able to show you."

Masha liked to climb trees; she quickly scrambled up among the big tree's branches and had soon pulled down all the apples from the tree.

"Ah," said the tree as she climbed down. "That feels so good. Thank you, little human. The *Gusi-lebedi* flew that way," added the tree, its branches bending to point the way.

Masha thanked the apple tree and set off again. She ran and she walked. She walked and she ran. The forest became darker and stranger.

Masha came across a pillar of stones. A similar one lay toppled on the ground not far away. The pillar that still stood held the rotten remains of a wooden gate—there had once been a house there. Up ahead, through the twisted trunks of the trees, Masha saw a patch of white; curiously she went to investigate. It was an oven, standing quite alone in the forest; its whitewash still bright in the shadows of the leaves.

"Ah, little girl, it is so good to see a human again," said the oven, its voice sad with loneliness. "Where are you going so deep in this forest?"

"Please, *Matushka-Pechka*," pleaded Masha, "tell me where the *Gusi-lebedi* have taken my little brother."

"Oh dear, oh dear, oh dear," fretted Mother-Stove, sounding like Masha's mother. "My child, I am so cold—there is no fire inside me. There are some fire stones up on my top shelf. Please help me light my fires, and I will tell you where you might find the *Gusi-lebedi*."

Masha found the stones and, after gathering some wood from the forest, quickly had a cheery fire blazing in the oven.

"Ah," sighed the oven, "that feels better. An oven without a fire is like a house without a family. Now, little girl, here is where you might find Babba Yagga and her *Gusi-lebedi*."

Masha thanked Mother-Stove, then she set off. Soon the forest became very dark and very strange. The gnarled trees stretched and spread their branches high and wide, so that, although it was well past noon, almost no light reached the path. In this twilight world beneath the leaves, Masha began to feel scared. She was tired and her feet hurt, but she went on, determined to find her brother.

Then, through the gloom beneath the trees, Masha saw an eerie line of lights. Swallowing her fear, she crept toward them. At the edge of a small clearing, she saw what could only have been Babba Yagga's home. The yard was surrounded by a fence, and atop the stakes, human skulls had been set, some large, some small—child-like. Sickly green-yellow beams of light shone from their eyeless sockets—it had been these eldritch lanterns that Masha had spotted from the forest.

Beyond the gruesome fence, she saw the roof of a small log hut. The logs of the side walls angled steeply back, while the eaves of the steep pitched roof swept up to the peak, making the roof seem much taller than the rest of the house. From the peak, a horse's skull hung, emitting its own ghostly light into the yard, hidden behind the fence. Masha, though frightened, crept closer, until she was at the side of Babba Yagga's yard.

Peering through the fence, Masha was relieved to see her brother, unharmed, playing on a bench beside the porch of the hut. Behind her brother on his bench, sat a large stone pot, large enough to stand in, and against this leaned a stout twig broom. Then Masha noticed that the hut, which had at first seemed to be set on poles holding it above the ground, was, in fact, held up by a pair of spindly chicken legs as tall as Masha. To her horror, as she watched, the legs shifted, causing the whole hut to twist and move.

There was the sound of something crashing to the floor inside the hut, and from inside came a string of cursing

and swearing, in a harsh high-pitched voice, accompanied by the loud stamping of someone's shoes on the floor. An ancient woman came out onto the porch, looking quite cross and, despite her obvious age, moving quickly without a cane or stick. She was as thin as a sapling, and her arms seemed too long for her body. She wore no kerchief, and her head was covered with a thinning pate of straggly hair, as white as chalk. Her face was lined with age beyond belief, and from her knobby chin, a few long white whiskers grew. Above a great hooked and wart-covered nose, a pair of eyes—as sharp as flint—flashed with both wisdom and malice as she gave the floor of the porch another stamp. The hut, on its bizarre chicken legs, stood motionless now, and the woman—Babba Yagga—

turned her gaze upon Masha's brother. He continued to play, unaffected by the crone's outburst, and she was now watching him attentively, the way Masha had seen cats watching birds outside the window.

Having come so far, she could hardly go back, and the way the ancient Babba Yaga looked at her brother gripped Masha with dread, but seeing her now left Masha frozen in place. Then she heard a hiss and a honk from close behind her. Spinning around she looked straight into the eye of one of Babba Yagga's *Gusi-lebedi*. In fact, all seven of the frightful birds were there, and they began herding her toward the gate to the yard, all the while honking and hissing loudly. Once inside, Babba Yaga shooed the Swan-Geese away and looked at Masha, although not sternly, and with a certain amusement and a twinkle in her eyes. Nevertheless, Masha's heart pounded.

"Dobrogo Zdorovia, Babuchka," Masha said, wishing the grandmotherly old woman good health, trying to be both polite and brave. "I have come to take my brother home."

"You are such a brave little girl," cooed Babba Yagga. "You have come so far," she continued. "It is getting late though, child," she declared. "Come inside and try my porridge. I will prepare the bathhouse and a bed for you, and in the morning, you may leave with your brother."

Masha reluctantly followed Babba Yagga up the steps and into her hut. She was amazed to see that the hut was much bigger inside than it had looked from the outside, but tired and now very hungry, Masha went to the table and began to eat. Babba Yagga watched her for a while, with a strange and disturbing smile on her face, and then, without another word, left.

Masha discovered she was actually very hungry, and began spooning the thick porridge into her mouth greedily. She had not eaten much though, when a small brown mouse appeared upon the table. Sitting back on its haunches, the tiny creature spoke to Masha.

"Please," it squeaked, "may I have a spoonful of your porridge and a sip from your mug?"

Masha was still quite hungry, but took pity on the creature and shared her meal with it.

"Thank you," said the mouse, carefully wiping its whiskers clean. "Now please listen to me. Babba Yagga eats the children the *Gusi-lebedi* bring to her. She has gone to light a fire to cook you both. You must take your brother and run away from here."

Hearing this, Masha ran out of the hut, leaving her meal half eaten. She gathered her brother up in her arms, and dashed into the forest.

Not long after, Babba Yagga returned, to find her two meals gone.

"Ah!" she cried. "They've run away! *Moi Gusi-lebedi!* Go! Catch them and bring them back at once. If you don't, I will eat you for supper!"

Masha had walked and run, had run and walked, and had gone far, but was afraid to hear the Swan-Geese honking, high up in the sky, looking for them. It was getting cold and dark. They came upon the oven, and tired Masha collapsed on the ground beside it.

"Hello again, little girl," said Mother-Stove. "I am hot and happy now. Warm yourselves by me for a while. Do not worry about the *Gusi-lebedi,* I will blow smoke to hide you from them."

Masha curled up with her brother beside the oven and rested. While the fires of the stove softly burned, a thick layer of smoke covered the forest, and the Swan-Geese could not find them. Soon, rested and feeling better, she thanked Mother-Stove, and continued on her way.

Masha ran and then walked. She walked and then she ran. They were almost at home—the forest was now becoming more familiar—when the Swan-Geese found them once again. Like hawks, they dove out of the sky, snipping at Masha and her brother with their beaks. Just then, Masha came to the clearing with the apple tree.

"Please, Sister-Tree," she wept, "help us! Hide us."

"Of course," said the tree, then spread its branches wide, allowing Masha and her brother to climb up, then wrapping its boughs around them both. The Swan-Geese honked and circled the tree, but protected by the thick branches of the great tree, they could not get at the two children. As the sun touched the horizon, the Swan-Geese gave a last spiteful honk, and then flew off.

Masha thanked the tree and hurried off to get home before it was completely dark.

When her parents returned home with their bags filled with presents for both Masha and her brother, Masha was very glad. From that day on, Masha never again got upset when her mother seemed to spend more time with her brother. She helped her mother take care of him as much as she could, and the *Gusi-lebedi*—the Swan-Geese—never again appeared over Masha's home.

Author's Note

The story of the Swan-Geese is old, perhaps even predating medieval times, and comes from Western and Central Russia. This is a tale usually read by parents to little children. It forms a very important link to the ancient traditions of the Russian people.

The moral or lessons the tale tries to convey are: family values, helpfulness, politeness and courage. Though bearing a great resemblance to Hansel and Gretel's witch, or to Oz's Wicked Witch of The West, Babba Yagga is not a witch or even a human. She is, in fact, a nature goddess and appears quite often in Russian folklore. Sometimes, she is an evil antagonist, as in this tale, but she also appears as a helpful being who assists the heroes of Russian folklore. Also, in Russian mythology, the garden apple tree was considered a gift from the gods and a great treasure. The tree could help people directly, as in this story, or even provide magical apples of youth.

Glossary

Dobrogo Zdorovia Babuchka— literally, 'May you have good health, Grandmother.' This is a very formal, even old-fashioned greeting, similar to 'Good day to you,' or 'How do you do?'

Gusi-lebedi—Swan-Geese; Russian folklore often features animals which straddle the line between the human world and the world of nature—the wild, and elegant, swan mixed with the ordinary goose of a Russian farmyard.

Mashenki—Masha darling; a common Russian term of endearment, a contraction of Masha (the girl's name) and *Dushenkia,* which is translated generally as 'darling.'

Matushka-Pechka—the stove/ oven; though Masha often refers to it as 'stove,' it is more recognizable to Western eyes as a clay oven, a *Pechka.* In ancient Russia, the stove was the heart of the house, giving warmth and food. It was treated with great respect, so Masha calls it 'Mother-Stove,' or *Matushka-Pechka.*

Milaya Dochka—my sweet daughter

The Field of Boliauns

A Traditional Folktale of Leprechaun Mischief from Ireland

by Kathy Jessup

One fine day, Tom Fitzpatrick was enjoying his leisure, taking a lazy walk down a country lane. It was *Lady Day in Harvest*—a holiday celebrated throughout Ireland—and Tom was pleased to have some time all to himself. Suddenly, he heard a sound coming through the hedge—clack, clack, clickety-clack!

"What could it be?" Tom wondered. He tiptoed closer to have a look, putting his eye right up against a hole in the hedge. To his surprise, he saw a wee little man wearing a brown leather apron and a three-cornered hat. The man was sitting on a tiny stool, and he was using a hammer to fix the heel on a fairy-sized shoe. "Oh, what luck!" whispered Tom. "Could it be a *leprechaun* I've found? I've often heard tales of the wee folk, but I never really believed the tales until now."

Irish legends were full of stories about *leprechauns* and their gold. It was said that if you were lucky enough to catch a *leprechaun,* you could be rich for life! But you must never take your eyes off a *leprechaun* until the gold was in your hand, for they were tricky folk and not to be trusted.

Well, Tom figured he was a clever fellow, as clever as any *leprechaun* might be. He crept up, keeping his eyes fixed on the little man, and greeted him, "Blessings on your work, my good neighbour!"

"Thank you," replied the *leprechaun*. He kept tapping away on the shoe without looking up.

Tom moved in closer, getting ready to snatch the wee fellow, but all the while keeping his voice friendly. "What a shame you have to work on a holiday, and such a lovely day it is, to be sure. Why not put your tools down for the moment, and we'll enjoy a visit," he said.

The *leprechaun* turned and looked sharply at Tom. "It's no business of yours whether I work or not," he growled. "You should mind your own business. Look! While you've been bothering me, your father's cows have broken into the oats and knocked the corn all about in the field." The *leprechaun* pointed a finger over Tom's shoulder.

Tom started to turn his head to look ... but then he remembered about *leprechauns* and their tricks! Quick as a flash, he grabbed the little man and held him tightly in his fist.

"Show me your gold," Tom demanded, "or I'll keep you my prisoner forever!"

"Gold! What gold?" the *leprechaun* protested. "Look at me. There are patches on my *breeches* and holes in my *brogues*. Do I look like a man who has gold?"

Tom shook his head. "Everyone knows *leprechauns* have gold. You're just trying to trick me—and it won't work!"

The *leprechaun* begged and pleaded to be let go, but Tom held fast, keeping his eyes firmly on the little fellow.

Finally, after much twisting and turning, unable to escape, the *leprechaun* relented. "Ah Tom, my boy, I see you're too clever for me. You've got me beat and that's for sure. I guess I'll have to show you where my treasure is hidden."

With that, the *leprechaun* led Tom on a long walk. They traipsed over hills and under hedges, through ditches, and across a crooked bit of *bog*. Tom was beginning to think that perhaps the *leprechaun* was playing a trick on him after all. At last, after many hours of wandering, they came to a great field of *boliaun* weeds. The *leprechaun* pointed to one of the large yellow bushes. "Dig under that *boliaun* and you'll find your treasure. More gold than you can carry!" he promised Tom.

"Ah, no ... what bad luck!" said Tom. "My spade is at home. If I go fetch it, how will I ever remember this exact spot? There must be a million *boliaun* bushes in this field, and they all look the same!"

Then, clever Tom had an idea. Still keeping an eye on the *leprechaun,* he took off a bright red garter from one of his socks, and tied it to the *boliaun* bush. "Swear you'll not touch this garter while I'm off getting my spade," he demanded. The little man promised he wouldn't, and Tom knew that even though *leprechauns* were tricky folk, once they gave a promise they always kept their word.

"I suppose now that you know where the gold is, you'll have no further use of me?" asked the *leprechaun*.

Glossary

bog—a type of mossy wetland

boliaun—the Gaelic name for a plant known as ragwort or ragweed, long associated with fairy folk

breeches—short pants that come to the knee

brogues—low-heeled shoes made of heavy leather

Lady Day in the Harvest— a holiday celebrating the Virgin Mary of the Catholic faith

leprechaun—an Irish fairy

"Well, now," said Tom, "since I have my fortune, I guess you can leave. May good luck go with you." Tom gently set the little man down on the ground.

As soon as he was free, the *leprechaun* smiled and his eyes began to twinkle. He danced away, calling over his shoulder, "Good-bye to you, Tom Fitzpatrick … may you do much good with what you find."

Tom immediately raced home to get his spade. All the way there and all the way back, his head was swimming with ideas of what he could do with his pile of gold. But when he arrived at the field of *boliauns*, an unusual sight met his eyes. Lo and behold, every *boliaun* bush was tied up with a red garter— identical to the one Tom owned. "Ah, no," he cried. "It can't be!" Tom's heart sank as he realized that finding the gold would be an impossible task. Sadly, he gave up and headed home, knowing that this time the *leprechaun* had gotten the better of him.

Tom lived to be an old, old man, and over time he gained a reputation as a hard worker and a great storyteller. Still, wherever he went, Tom always kept a spade handy and an ear perked—listening for a clack, clack, clickety-clack! "Next time," vowed clever Tom, "should I ever meet a *leprechaun*, I will be ready!"

Author's Note

Thomas Crofton Croker first published this classic Irish folktale in his book, *Fairy Legends and Traditions of the South of Ireland,* in 1825. I remember hearing the story as a child, in a version called *Clever Tom and the Leprechaun.* While many cultures have fairy-type figures in their lore, the leprechaun is unique to Ireland. The idea of *luck* plays an important role in many Irish stories, as in the popular expression, "Luck of the Irish." There is a subtle moral lesson in this fairy story, as Tom's greed and mean treatment of the leprechaun leads to his just reward—going away with nothing!

Erla and the Raven

An Icelandic Tale
by Faye Mogensen

*A tumble of black, a raucous call, eyes that see all.
Who am I?*

Erla knew! Way out in the country, on the farm where she lived, there were lots of ravens. She loved watching them soar overhead.

Her farm was called *Feskuvatn,* named after the spring of fresh water that bubbled up from underground, and it was so far from neighbours that visitors rarely came. Still, Erla wasn't exactly lonely; the house was full to the brim with her parents and brothers, and the barn was crowded with animals, and her days were always busy.

Erla arose early each morning to tend the chickens and check on the sheep. She helped plant, weed, and harvest vegetables. She cooked meals, cleaned up, and helped shear, spin, weave, and stitch wool. She and her mother worked side by side from daybreak to nightfall, and yet it never felt like they were working. There was always time to stop and enjoy the day, and to marvel at the rugged and wild landscape of the *Vatnsdalur*—the valley in northwest Iceland that nestled their farm. It was the kind of place that filled your head with dreams, and Erla liked to dream a lot.

Sometimes it was the clouds overhead that inspired her. Other times it was the craggy landscape, or the eerie sound of the wind. But most often, it was the birds soaring overhead that launched Erla into one of her daydreams.

Erla imagined a raven perching upon her shoulder. In her mind, she stroked its gleaming black feathers, and told the dark beauty all her secrets. She shared food with it, and 'saw' one eating right from her hand. The more Erla dreamed about it, the more she wanted to tame a raven!

Her father was quite the opposite; he despised the birds. If 'a tumble of black' flew overhead, her father would shoo it away. If 'a raucous call' approached the barn, he'd roar. If 'the eyes that see all' appeared to glance at the well, he'd begin to throw rocks. Her father did not like to share that fine spring water with relatives or neighbours, let alone a raven!

Erla could not understand him. The ravens meant no harm! And the more her father grumbled about them, the more Erla's heart reached out to them. One day at dinner, she summoned all her courage, and when no one was looking, she scraped a few crumbs of salt fish from her plate into her handkerchief. There was little food to spare, but Erla wanted to share!

She wrapped that treasure tightly, thrust it into her apron pocket, and when

she'd finished her chores and her father lay in his bed enjoying an afternoon nap, she snuck up onto the rise behind the farmyard. There, she laid the food scraps on a large rock, offering them to the ravens.

The ravens didn't come … not at first.

Everyone knows that ravens do not associate with people, but Erla didn't give up! Each and every day, she hid small crusts of bread, spoonfuls of porridge or pieces of roast mutton in her handkerchief and placed them into her pocket. She carried her treasures up the hill to the same large rock and left them there.

Eventually, she noticed that a raven had caught on. And after that, she began to perch upon the rock beside the scraps of food. She enjoyed the views from there. Looking to the south, she could see mountains so high, they seemed to touch the sky. To the north, sometimes there was a bit of haze over the distant sea. But most of the time, her eyes were focused upward, hoping for jet-black wings; and her ears were wide open, wishing for the sound of a rollicking and raucous call.

Eventually, the raven even dared to come while she sat there! Erla couldn't believe her good fortune. She stayed as still as the rocks around her. She waited and waited. The raven hopped beside her, and at last, pecked at the morsel of food before flying off.

As the days went by, Erla set the food down closer and closer to her hand until finally, she didn't set it on the rock—she held the tidbit in her hand. On that miraculous day, the raven bent down and took it right from her hand! The brush of his strong, ebony bill tickled her skin and her fancy. Erla's dream was coming true!

Not long after, she began placing the food upon her shoulder. The raven was quick to notice, and only a little slower to work up the courage to perch there, with his glossy black wings close to Erla's cheek. The girl was completely captivated. She gave her new friend the name 'Hrafn.' Life was good!

Luckily, Erla's father slept deeply, her brothers didn't pay any attention and her mother was fond of birds. If her father happened to awaken early from his nap, her mother was quick to distract him with tea or talk, so that Erla's daily ritual was never discovered. That was quite a feat, because it went on for years! Each and every day, summer and winter, from about the age of eight, she made her trip up to the rise and was rewarded with a peck on the hand, a perch on the shoulder, and sometimes an athletic display of aerial acrobatics.

Many autumns later, when Erla was a young woman of 16 years, Hrafn surprised her. After swallowing the food she brought, he flew off without perching on her shoulder. Without offering a single loop-de-loop! He just plain disappeared.

Erla was alarmed. Was her father approaching? She looked all around, then sighed with relief—that wasn't it. And soon enough, Hrafn returned. This time, he perched upon her shoulder, but only for a split second before he flew off again—without first releasing his talons. It was as though he was trying to pull her with him. Then he was gone.

"What are you doing, Hrafn?" she called. He returned a third time, and this time he grabbed at Erla's skirt before flying off.

"Oh! You want me to fly with you," she laughed, "I will!" She spread her arms wide open and broke into a run. She ran so swiftly across that smooth firm ground that she felt like she was flying. Her skirts flapped all around her, her hair danced in the wind behind her.

They ran on and on, higher and higher up the mountain. Erla was puffing and panting. She slowed down, leaned back her head and called out, "Kwaaa, kwaaa, kwaaa!" Hrafn replied with a lovely, "Kluuk, kluuk. Kluuk, kluuk!"—the true call of friendship. And they 'flew' on.

Higher and higher they went and, just when Erla was beginning to feel she could run no further, Hrafn swooped down to perch on the craggy rock that rose there from the mountain. Stretching and straining, Erla clambered up to join him. She was worn out, but excited to be there! She'd never been so high up the mountain before.

She had almost caught her breath when, suddenly, everything shifted. There was a great rumbling sound. Erla looked around nervously. It wasn't her father, it was far worse! Below her, rocks had begun to roll.

Erla remembered seeing small landslides as a child. But this one was different. She clung tightly to the craggy rock upon which she sat, and watched in horror as rocks and clay rushed down the mountainside. Then, as suddenly as it all began, everything was still and silent; everything, except her heart which would not stop pounding.

In amazement, Erla realized that the bedrock beneath her was solid. It was like a lifeboat, barely above a river of putty. She looked at Hrafn in wonder—he had led her to safety! How had he known?

And then, though she hardly dared, Erla turned to look toward the farm. No matter how hard she squinted or stared, she could not see a single building—there were only rocks and rubble. She worried—and then remembered how far she had run. Maybe the farm was just too far away to see.

She scrambled back down from the rocks and tried to run again. Hope was in her heart, but her legs were heavy, and all the debris tripped her and slowed her down.

At long last, Erla arrived in the hollow where the farm should have been. There was no hint of a house or a barn, only rubble and ruin, and what looked like a sod roof, except that it was on the ground. She began to call, *"Móðir! Faðir! Móðir! Bjarni! Fridrik! Halldor! Faðir! Móðir! Mó-ó-óðir!"*

She would have been relieved to hear her father's stern voice that day. She would have been happy if her brothers began to tease her. She would have been overjoyed by the sound of her mother's gentle voice. But no one was there. Nothing. The air was still and silent. Erla stumbled on, almost in a trance. She knew she needed help. She knew she had to go to the nearest neighbour.

Her only companions on that dark, narrow trail were a half-moon and the faithful Hrafn, who circled overhead while she stumbled below. The path felt endless; until, just as the sun came up, Erla crumpled at the door to the neighbour's farmhouse.

Inside the house, they were startled by the noise. Svein opened the door cautiously. When he saw it was Erla, he picked her up in his arms, and with a nod of approval from his mother, placed her on the day bed and covered her with a quilt.

Erla's father had never so much as lent a pair of shears to Svein's family; he'd never shared a drop of that fine spring water. But they would help Erla—she was a neighbour girl in need. And they knew what had happened—the rumble of the landslide had been so loud that they had heard it too.

The next morning, Svein and his brothers hurried up the hill toward *Feskuvatn,* returning later that day, with long, sad faces. They had seen no sign of any of Erla's family.

So, a new life began for Erla. She was made welcome at meal times and given the day bed to call her own. She worked hard and willingly, wherever and whenever she was needed. But she never said a word, nor did her face show any expression. It was as though the landslide had stolen her voice and her heart when it stole her family.

Erla continued her habit of scraping a few morsels of food from her plate into her handkerchief. When she had finished her chores, she would head up onto the rise above her new home and offer her gift to Hrafn. In this way, she seemed to find a quiet sort of contentment. With her new family, she didn't need to be secretive or worry—no one minded ravens. In fact, they were fascinated—especially Svein. Sometimes he followed Erla partway up the rise and watched in amazement as a raven swooped down to take food right out of her hand! He felt a little jealous when the raven perched upon her shoulder and rubbed her cheek with its glossy black wing. But he was happy when he saw Erla smile at her feathered friend.

All throughout winter, one day melted into another, each the same as the one before. When spring came at last, there was a shift. The young men grew busy, preparing to head to the greener pastures of the high country with the sheep and their few cows.

Off they went. Svein's brothers teased him for being distracted and dreamy. They told him that he was more interested in the ravens flying overhead than the ground beneath his feet. Then, as though to prove it, Svein lodged his foot in a hole and he tripped.

When Svein pulled his foot back out of the hole, he smelled something horrible! At first, he hurried away to join his brothers. But when he realized where he was—surrounded by the rubble and ruin of Erla's family farmstead—he rushed back to the hole, and called for his brothers' help.

They shifted boulder after boulder away from that hole. They moved rocks and stones and rubble, until the hole was large enough for Svein to drop down inside. He was scared to do it, but he had to know what was down there.

When his eyes adjusted to the dark, he could scarcely believe what he saw! There were crocks, like the ones his mother filled with salt fish and meat. There were baskets, like the ones where his mother stored grain. This was a pantry! This must be the pantry at *Feskuvatn*.

Suddenly, he heard a noise behind him. Svein gasped. He hoped it was a rat. But, no … it was a skeleton! Except that it couldn't be a skeleton—it was moving. It was reaching its arms out toward Svein and it was moaning.

Svein wanted to fly from that place! Instead, he summoned up all his courage, walked toward the movement and picked up that sack of bones. He pushed it up out of the opening through which he'd dropped down. Once he'd crawled back out, he saw the tattered skirt and long hair. It was a woman! He picked her back up and began to run down the slopes toward home. Fast and furious, he ran on and on.

Erla happened to be out working in the garden. It was Hrafn who first caught her eye. What was he doing here, so early in the day? Then she saw Svein. Why was he returning and what was he carrying? As he came closer, Erla couldn't stop herself, she began to run toward him. When she saw that thin figure of a woman, she pulled her into her arms,

GLOSSARY

Erla—a popular Icelandic girl's name

Faðir—father

Feskuvatn—the fictitious name of the farm; means 'fresh water'

Hrafn—the raven's name; the Icelandic word for 'raven'

Móðir—mother

Svein, Bjarni, Fridrik, Halldor —Icelandic boys' names

Vatnsdalur—the name of the valley; means 'water valley'

and rocked her back and forth, and back and forth. Then, for the first time since the landslide she spoke, *"Móðir! Móðir!"* Her voice cracked, "You're alive!"

Overhead, Hrafn did a loop-de-loop. Beside her, Svein smiled. And at that moment, Erla knew. She knew that she would marry Svein.

Before that, they would all go to *Feskuvatn* to search again for the rest of her family. What they would find, she was not sure, but Erla had new hope in her heart. And whatever happened, they would rebuild the old farmhouse. They would find the spring and build a solid well around it. When the water bubbled up they would share it with their relatives and neighbours, and with the ravens, "Kwaaa-Kwaaa-Kwaaak!"

That is the true story of Erla and the raven.

AUTHOR'S NOTE

My heritage is both Danish and Icelandic, and when my Icelandic friend, Ingibjörg Gisladottir, heard that I was looking for Nordic stories about ravens, she shared this tale with me. I have been told that it is well known in Iceland and can be found in Icelandic on the Internet. Despite searching many collections of Icelandic folktales published in English, I have not yet found it. In one of the versions I have been told, it was a priest who found the mother. I took the liberty of choosing to make the character the young neighbour. The story takes place a few hundred years ago, on the eastern slopes of the Vatnsdalur in northwestern Iceland. It is an area shaped by numerous landslides, known to have taken many lives over the centuries. At the time of the story and in that rugged place, a young girl may well have enjoyed an animal's friendship; their intimate relationship reflects the typically close tie to nature experienced by Icelanders. In the story, the strong Icelandic community values are reflected when Erla's kindness and generosity are rewarded. I was drawn to the story, because it suggests that we can learn from the wisdom of wild animals.

The story's introductory riddle alludes to the tradition of 'kenning,' or condensed metaphors, typically used in the ancient skaldic poems of Iceland. Usually composed of only two words, 'kennings' were sometimes extended into phrases, and always described things in an unusual way.

Mischief and the Moon

A Folktale from Japan
by Nathalie Vachon

A long time ago, when the Earth was new, there was no moon and in certain pockets of the world there was unrest. Having no moon especially affected the Japanese people because when the sun sank into the Sea of Japan and the night sky echoed with darkness, the Shadow Gods, the *Kuragari,* came out and did a trance dance sending everyone into a deep, deep sleep. And there was only one purpose for this dance: to prepare the air for mischief!

And did those Shadow Gods ever get into some serious mischief! The next morning when the sun came up, the people who didn't make it home on time the night before would find themselves waking up in the middle of a rice field or half-way home from an elder's house. They would find that their houses had been transported to another prefecture, or the *tatami* mats were stacked up outside like playing cards, or the cows were in the fields wearing *kimono.* This caused quite a disruption in the lives of the Japanese people. So, they did what they always did for matters of such importance. They called the Goddess of Harmony, Chowa-san, down from her mountaintop to chair a meeting. Chowa-san sat there in her long flowing kimono, her black hair streaked with silver and her eyes twinkling with wisdom, and she listened … and she listened … and she listened … to the concerns of the Japanese people. At the end of the meeting it was agreed that what they needed was a great lantern in the sky to scare away those shadows of the night.

That afternoon, Chowa-san returned to her mountain and created an especially large fire. And into that fire she threw a magic ball, which burned and burned and burned until there was nothing left but a big ball of glowing embers. That evening, as the sun sank into the Sea of Japan and the night sky echoed with darkness, she said the words:

> *Hikari akari miyo no sekai*
> *We're in need of your light to shine in the sky.*

With those words she launched the ball, and it went up and up and up until it was suspended there by the darkness.

Well, that night the Shadow Gods did not come out. And the night after that, the Shadow

Gods did not come out. And the night after that, the Shadow Gods did not come out. And everyone thought their problems were solved, but there was still one problem, the people went from sleeping all night long to not sleeping at all. This ball of light in the sky filled their bones with so much energy that they were compelled to stay up all night and create their own mischief.

Chowa-san saw this and thought, "Things are not in balance." So that afternoon she went to the top of her mountain, selected an especially large branch from a cherry blossom tree, and began to carve and carve and carve until she had a long, slightly curved shape. And that evening, as the sun sank into the Sea of Japan, she said the words:

> *Hikari akari miyo no sekai*
> *I must cover some of your light that shines in the sky.*

With those words she launched that branch and it went up and up and up until it covered a portion of that glowing ball. Well, that night the energy of the people died down a bit. But the Shadow Gods noticed that something was going on and peeked their heads up to see what it was.

Chowa-san saw this happening and thought, "Things are still not in balance." So that afternoon she went to the top of her mountain, selected another especially large branch from a cherry blossom tree, and began to carve and carve and carve until she had a long, slightly curved shape. And that evening, as the sun sank into the Sea of Japan, she said the words:

> *Hikari akari miyo no sekai*
> *I must cover some of your light that shines in the sky.*

With those words she launched that branch and it went up and up and up until it covered an even larger portion of that glowing ball. Well, that night the energy of the people died down a little more. But the Shadow Gods noticed how dark it was getting and came up, fully prepared for mischief.

Chowa-san saw that this was happening and thought, "Things are still not in balance." So, again she went to the top of her mountain, she selected one large branch, she said the words *Hikari akari miyo no sekai*, and she launched that branch up into the sky.

But this night something different happened: this night, that lantern shone half dark and half bright and the people and the Shadow Gods joined in the dance of mischief. Every night, Chowa-san kept covering the lantern till it became dark again and then after some days she brought up the complete bright lantern again. This way, people would dance some nights and sleep other nights.

Now some say that to this day you can still see Chowa-san on the top of her mountain maintaining harmony for the people of Japan. And to this day, she'll still have visitors who travel far and wide to ask her one very important question. They bow and say, "Excuse me Chowa-san, but if it is balance that you seek, why not create a moon that shines half dark and half bright each and every night?"

And with this question, Chowa-san's laughter streaks the sky and she replies, "My friend, balance comes from allowing the times when the Shadow Gods drain the energy from our bones as well as the times when we are filled with energy and compelled to create our own mischief. Balance comes from embracing both the light and the dark, and anyway, my good friend … life is more fun that way."

AUTHOR'S NOTE

This folktale was written by Nathalie after her experience of living in Osaka, Japan. The story embraces many qualities of Japanese culture, such as harmony, group decision making, and the importance of tradition along with a reverence and an honouring of nature and elders. The story teaches us that balance comes from embracing all the cycles or stages of life.

The Squire's Bride

A Norwegian Folktale
by Pearl-Ann Gooding

In a time long past, a Squire in Norway lived only to serve his king. He fought for many years at his king's side, both on the seas and on the land. The frigid northern waters, rugged mountains, and vast forests were easily navigated and managed by the hardy and seasoned servant. The king acknowledged his great service with lands, titles, gold, silver, and all manner of precious stones. The Squire became richer and richer, yet he cared not. His road was for adventure and service to his king.

His friends would tell him over and over that he should find peace and take rest. He should take himself a bride and have a family. But the Squire would not listen to their counsel. Over the years, each of his friends found wives and had many children. Then when their children began to have children, he took note. He began to realize all the years that had gone by, and that all the lands, titles, and wealth he had gained would be lost, as he had no one to leave them to. He thought—for the first time—perhaps he should take a bride.

He had no idea how to court for he had never before taken an interest in it. Now it seemed foolish for a man his age to think of courting and wooing a young woman. The thought almost terrified him. As a matter of fact, he would have much rather been on the front lines of a battle than seeking out a bride.

One day, as he looked out over his lands—seeing the beauty and richness of the valley as the crops were fed by the Glanna River—he noticed the farmer's daughter working in the fields. She was certainly a comely girl, and no doubt she was strong and healthy. Granted, she was far beneath his social status, but because of that,

there would be no need to court her. He would just take her as a bride, she would be happy and all would be well. He walked out to her in the field and asked her, "Do you know who I am, child?"

"*Ja, min herre.* Yes, my lord," she replied.

"*Svaert god.* Very good," said he. "As you know, I am a great lord with many lands and titles, but have no wife."

"*Ja, min herre,*" she acknowledged.

"I have decided to take a bride," he announced.

"*Oh, hvarden fantastishk!* Oh, how wonderful!" the farmer's daughter exclaimed. "I am so happy for you and how blessed she will be!"

"Indeed," said the Squire, "that is good, for I have decided that you will be my bride!"

"*Meg?* Me? Oh, my lord, I do thank you for your generous offer, but I do not know you nor do I love you," she meekly replied. She thought, "Is he crazy? He is an old man and I am a young woman. He is old enough to be my father!"

At first, he thought perhaps she didn't understand exactly what it was he was offering. He kindly explained, "My dear, all these lands and manors will become yours if you become mistress. You and any children you bear will never suffer or want for anything."

"*Ja, min herre.* I do realize this great gift that you are offering, but … but, I do not love you," she replied.

The Squire thought perhaps she was a bit addled in the brain and decided that he would speak to her father instead.

He found the farmer and explained to him that he had decided to take a bride and that his eye had fallen upon the farmer's daughter. The farmer was thrilled.

"You wish to marry my daughter? This is so wonderful!" exclaimed the farmer.

"Ja," said the Squire, "but I have spoken to her, and she said she would not have me because she does not love me, so I have come to you."

The farmer's countenance fell, "Did she say she will not have you?" he asked sadly.

The Squire nodded.

"Oh," said the farmer, "if she said she would not have you, then I will not force her."

The Squire could hardly believe his ears, "Are you serious, man?" he asked. "Do you know what it is that I offer? To your daughter—a farmer's daughter—I offer the station of mistress of all that I own. She will want for nothing all her days. Her children will be secure in lands and wealth and you … you will be given this parcel of land that you have worked all these years, as a bride's price."

"Would I own my own land?" the farmer asked incredulously. He had never dared to imagine that he would ever own anything, let alone his own piece of land. And to know that his daughter and grandchildren to come would never want for anything made his heart soar. "I am sure that once I have spoken to her, my lord, she will see reason and accept your hand."

"Svaert god," said the Squire, "Should I plan for the wedding day?"

"Ja, min herre. She will marry you," the farmer confirmed.

"I will set the date for a fortnight and expect to collect her then," said the Squire.

The farmer went in search of his daughter and found her still working hard in the field. "Daughter," he called, "I have spoken to the Squire, and he desires to marry you!"

"Jeg vet Far! I know, Father! Can you imagine?" she cried. "A young woman like me, marry him, an old man! I don't even know him—how could I marry him?"

"But daughter, look at what it is that he offers you. Mistress of all that he owns—you will want for nothing! Your children, heirs to greatness, and I, a poor farmer, will be given my own parcel of land!" explained the farmer.

"Oh, Far. Oh, Father," said the daughter, "would you sell me for a plot of land?"

The farmer shook his head sadly, "No, daughter, if you will not have him, I will not force you."

The farmer then turned to go to the manor house to tell the Squire that the wedding would not be. To this news, the Squire would neither listen nor would he agree.

"You gave me your word!" exclaimed the Squire. "I have already made arrangements—the wedding will take place," he said firmly.

"But … she will not have you," pleaded the farmer.

"If you go back on your word, I will throw you off my lands and make sure that no one will take you in," threatened the Squire. "You and your daughter will starve and die! You *will* see that this marriage *does* take place," retorted the Squire.

"Jeg ser. I see," said the farmer, "My daughter will marry you."

Sadly, the farmer turned around and went back home. He didn't know how to tell his daughter. Each time he saw her, he tried to tell her, but each time he couldn't find the words. Soon the two weeks had passed, and still he hadn't told his daughter.

The day of the wedding arrived. The Squire called for one of the stable boys to go to the farmer's house and to get from the farmer what had been promised to him on his wedding day. So, the young boy went to the farmer. He knocked on the door, and when the farmer answered, the boy told him he was there to get what had been promised the Squire on his wedding day. The farmer looked out into the field and saw his daughter. He pointed to her, and told the boy to go out and fetch her. The stable boy went into the field to the farmer's

daughter and told her that he had come to get what her father had promised the Squire on his wedding day.

The daughter was very quick-minded and knew exactly what had happened, but would not be taken in. Quickly she said, "Are you to pick up what my father has promised the Squire on his wedding day?"

"Ja," said the stable boy.

"Very well then," said she as she turned and pointed to the old grey mare that was grazing out in the field. "Go and get her, that is what my father has promised the Squire."

The stable boy grabbed a rope and looped it around the mare's neck and led her up to the manor house. He then tied her to the back door and went inside to find the Squire.

"Well boy, do you have her?" asked the Squire.

"Ja, min herre," answered the boy.

"Where is she?" the Squire asked.

"I tied her up at the back door," the boy replied.

"You tied her up at the back door?" exclaimed the Squire.

"Ja, min herre, I didn't want her to run away," said the stable boy.

"Well, bring her in, boy! Take her up to mother's chambers," ordered the Squire.

"Do you want me to bring her up to your mother's chambers, Squire?" asked the boy in amazement.

"Are you deaf, boy?" asked the Squire, "Yes, bring her up to my mother's chambers!"

"But, my lord ... I don't think I can get her up there by myself," he stammered.

"Then run to the stable and get some more men to help you. I want her up there right away!" commanded the Squire.

The stable boy ran out to the stables and gathered three other workers to come and help him. They took the mare through the kitchen and then up the back stairs to the appointed room. It took a lot of energy—there was pushing and pulling, grunting and groaning—but finally, she was in. The stable boy ran back to report to the Squire.

"Is she in the room?" asked the Squire. With sweat running down his face, the boy nodded his head.

"Good, now go to the kitchen and tell the maids to go upstairs and give her a bath. I want flowers in her hair, a veil on her head and the wedding dress placed on her," said the Squire.

"Do you want the maids to bathe her? … put flowers in her hair? … a veil on her head? And … and the wedding dress on her?" the young boy questioned.

"JA!" yelled the Squire. "I want it done immediately!" he roared.

The stable boy ran into the kitchen, called the young maids and told them what to do. The girls clapped their hands in delight! "Does this mean that this whole wedding is a jest?" they exclaimed. "All the years that the Squire's friends have pushed him to marry—and now he has finally made all the plans, ordered the feast, invited the guests, brought in the minister—and all for a jest!" The girls laughed, "Never will they push the Squire again!" They ran out of the kitchen and up the stairs, giggling all the way, to be a part of such a wonderful plot.

It was a difficult chore to be sure, but the girls made sure that all was perfect. Then they ran down to report to the Squire.

"Is she ready?" asked the Squire.

"She is ready, my lord," replied one of the young maids.

"Did you give her a bath?" the Squire asked.

"Ja, min herre," the maid answered.

"Has she flowers in her hair?" he questioned.

The girls nodded, with big grins across their faces.

"Did you place the veil upon her head?" the Squire asked.

Again, the girls nodded and giggled, covering their mouths with their fingers.

"She is wearing the wedding dress?" he asked.

"Ja, min herre," the girls replied, just beaming with delight.

"Then bring her down and let the ceremony begin!" the Squire called out.

The girls ran upstairs, and the Squire called to all of his guests to gather around. He invited the minister to stand beside him at the front of the great hall, as they waited for the bride to enter. All eyes were turned toward the chamber door, with the Squire and minister waiting expectantly at the front.

The door opened and the mare came out. Sure enough, there were flowers in her hair, a veil upon her head, and the wedding dress on her horse body!

The entire room was silent, except for the clip-clop of the mare's hooves as she made her way down the hall, and down the stairs to where the Squire stood. The Squire's face had fallen and his mouth dropped open. No one could see the look of astonishment on his face, save his chosen bride.

Finally, an old friend came forward and slapped the Squire on the back. "You old fool!" he laughed, "You had us all believing that this was a real wedding … that you had finally come to your senses!" Then the whole room broke out in laughter.

The Squire, too, began to chuckle. "Yes, I had you all fooled, didn't I?" he said.

Well, they all ate, drank, and made merry. As for the Squire … well, the Squire never went courting again!

Author's Note

The Squire's Bride, I imagine, takes place in the milder and more fertile lowlands of the country of Norway. The tale or *eventyr* as it is called, probably wandered back to Norway during the Middle Ages. Norwegian folktales contain an undertone of realism and humour that makes them unique. This tale reflects the tremendous imagination of the Norwegian people, as well as their independence and self-reliance. The farmer's daughter, in this story, stands up for her choice and defeats the Squire very subtly. I took special interest in this tale when looking for empowering stories from common folk while I was preparing for a series of Hutterite Colony Storytelling Tours.

Anansi and the Turtle

A Folktale from Senegal
by Estelle Salata

After a long hot day under the African sun, Anansi the spider sat down to eat his dinner. That afternoon he had caught some fish in the Ankobra River, and to accompany them, he had plucked yams straight from the warm rich earth. He could hardly wait. The first forkful of food was halfway to his mouth when he heard a knock on the door.

"Who is it?" Anansi asked in a rude voice, for he disliked being disturbed when he was eating.

"It is your friend, Turtle."

"Just a minute," said Anansi. He put down his fork and went to open the door. He saw Turtle standing on the mat. What do you want?"

"I was just travelling on your side of the river, my friend," said Turtle. "I've been walking since early morning and I'm tired and hungry."

Anansi stared at him a moment.

Turtle's heavily lidded eyes popped open when he caught sight of the delicious food on Anansi's table.

"Oh, I see that you were about to eat dinner," said Turtle, his mouth watering at the sight of steaming yams on a platter. "Don't let me stop you, Anansi."

"Come inside and share my food," said Anansi, none too pleased with the unexpected company. But in Africa, it is considered rude and ill-mannered to turn a stranger or a friend away from the door without first inviting him to dinner.

Turtle hurried over to the table and sat down opposite Anansi. He was about to begin eating when Anansi scowled at him.

"Oh, how dreadful," said Anansi in a shocked voice. He wrinkled up his nose in distaste. "I've just noticed how dirty your hands and feet are, Turtle. Here on this side of the Ankobra River, it is considered extremely bad manners for a guest to come to the table with dirty feet. There is a stream at the bottom of the hill. Do you mind washing yourself before you eat?"

Poor Turtle was so hungry he didn't know how he could wait any longer. Anansi was shovelling the yams into his own mouth as quickly as possible. If Turtle didn't hurry, Anansi would surely have everything eaten in no time.

Turtle nodded, then plodded as fast as he could down the dirt path to the stream to wash his feet. When they were clean, he trudged back up the hill to Anansi's table. Anansi was still busy gobbling down his dinner. It was already half gone.

"Turtle," admonished Anansi, looking at him with distaste, "your hands and feet are just as dirty and dusty as they were before. I thought I asked you to wash them."

"I did," said Turtle, extremely embarrassed, "but your trail is dusty. My feet became dirty again when I walked up the path."

"Well, don't expect to eat with me until they are absolutely clean," said Anansi, stuffing a huge portion of fish into his mouth.

Once again, Turtle shuffled down the path to the stream. He carefully washed his hands and feet. This time he was careful not to step on the path but walked on the clean grass beside it. He arrived at the table just as Anansi was wiping his mouth with a napkin.

"Ah, that was a delightful meal even if I do say so myself," Anansi said when he saw Turtle. "It is too bad, my friend, that you couldn't find the time to share my dinner with me."

"That's quite all right," said Turtle stiffly. "I hope that someday, Anansi, I can return the favour to you."

"Oh, it is nothing, nothing," said Anansi. "Think nothing of it. My home is open to everyone."

One hot afternoon several months later, Anansi found himself on Turtle's side of the Ankobra River. He had spent the entire day scuttling and scurrying back and forth through the tall grasses, and had not found anything to eat since breakfast. He was hot and tired and hungry. When he reached Turtle's house, he found him sunning himself in the mud beside a small pond.

"Good afternoon, Anansi," said Turtle cordially. "You certainly look tired. Have you been travelling long?"

"All day," said Anansi, feeling sorry for himself. "I was hoping that I could reach your house before dark."

"You have timed your visit perfectly," said Turtle. "I have just prepared my evening meal down at the bottom of the pond. Please come and join me. I remember well your hospitality the day that I visited you in your country."

Anansi smiled, pleased. Turtle waded into the water and plunged to the bottom. Although Anansi didn't care too much for water, he forced himself to follow, his spiky arms and legs flailing in all directions as he tumbled and toppled to the bed of the pool.

Anansi's eyes nearly popped out of his bald head. There, spread before him on a clean, white tablecloth was the most delicious meal he had ever seen—platters of fresh seafood, shrimp, eel, fish, and clams. Anansi couldn't wait!

"Help yourself," said Turtle, chewing his food slowly.

Just as Anansi was about to sit down at the table, he began floating upward. He glided slowly to the surface, as his skinny arms and legs were too frail to keep him on the bottom.

Anansi bobbed around in the water, then wriggled his way to land. On the banks, he scampered and scrambled back and forth, trying to figure out a way to reach the bottom of the pond before the food was gone. Then, he had a brilliant idea! He shuttled about the rocks and filled the pockets of his jacket with pebbles to weigh him down.

Again, he tumbled into the water and sank straight to the bottom. Turtle, eating slowly but steadily, had already polished off half the contents of the platters.

"Ah, there you are, Anansi," said Turtle pleasantly. "I thought you had gone home. Help yourself. There is plenty of food here for both of us."

Anansi, his mouth watering, was about to pick up his fork when Turtle stopped him. "I'm so sorry, Anansi," he explained, "but on my side of the Ankobra River it is considered ill-mannered to come to the table wearing a jacket. Will you kindly remove your jacket before you eat?"

Eagerly, Anansi squirmed out of his jacket. As soon as he had removed the coat, he began to float away from the table. Up, up, he went, to the top of the water.

"Where are you going, Anansi?" asked Turtle, as Anansi floundered about, kicking his arms and legs until he was out of sight. "It is considered rude on my side of the river to leave the table before the meal is over."

"But I don't want to leave yet," cried Anansi, as he spluttered to the surface. "I'm still hungry."

"Share and share alike, I always say," Turtle gurgled from the bottom of the pond. "Do come and visit me again soon, Anansi. It's been a pleasure having such a fine guest to dinner."

AUTHOR'S NOTE

Anansi the spider is the favourite hero of the Ashanti people living in the Gold Coast in West Africa. Folktales about this wily trickster, who outwits others only to have the tables turned on him, are known as *Anansesem* or spider tales. Traditionally, the *Anansesem* are told only after dark. Anansi's fame has spread throughout West Africa and as far away as the Congo region. Centuries ago, when the Africans were sent to the New World as slaves, they brought their Anansi tales with them. The stories are told in the United States, in many islands of the West Indies, and in South America This story of Anansi and the Turtle points out the emphasis the people of Africa place on cleanliness. They bathe in hot water before they begin their day's work, and again in the evening when they have returned from their daily tasks. One of the values in Anansi tales shows the importance the African culture places on cleanliness before eating. The moral of the story warns readers that what goes around, comes around. Or, as you do unto others, so shall it be done unto you.

The Girl Who Married the Morning Star

A BLACKFOOT TALE

BY MARY HAYS AND LOUIS SOOP

Long, long ago in a far off place …

Three girls were sleeping out under the stars. They dozed, and talked, and looked at the stars above. They talked about who they would marry. They thought about the young men they knew. They talked of one who was tall and handsome, of one who had long, black braids, and of one who had a nice smile and gentle eyes.

But none of the young men pleased the eldest girl, the chief's daughter. When dawn's first light was about to break over the horizon and the morning star shone brightly, one of the girls said, "No one pleases you. Perhaps you should marry that bright star; perhaps you should marry the Morning Star!"

The eldest replied, "The Morning Star is beautiful. I *wish* I could marry the Morning Star!"

When dawn broke, they rose, went back to their village, and went about their daily tasks.

Some time later the chief's daughter was out gathering firewood. She saw moccasins ahead of her on the path. When she looked up, to her surprise, there was a finely dressed, handsome young man. She was startled, but he spoke gently to her, "I am the Morning Star—*Aa pii so woh sa.* I am the one you called. I have come to take you as my wife and to take you to live with me in the Sky Country."

The girl took his hand and left her village behind. Morning Star was dressed in a beautiful feather cloak. He wrapped it around her and together they rose up into the sky, to the Sky Country.

The Sky Country was a wondrous place. There was no sickness and no hunger—there was enough food for all. The lodges never wore out and winter never came.

45

There was only the work one wished to do. When the hunting parties went out, if someone was injured, he would appear the next day healed. It was a wonderful life and the young couple knew great happiness. The girl learned various songs and ceremonies. She kept herself busy learning new things and she became very wise.

But each day when Morning Star went out, he said the same thing to her, "Do not pick the sacred turnip, the *Maas*." He said this to her each and every day and she followed his instructions. However, after some time, she began to think of nothing but the sacred turnip—the thought filled her every waking moment until she could stand it no longer. She went out and pulled and pulled the turnip, the *Maas*, until she pulled it right out. It left a hole in the sky, and when she looked through the hole, she could see down to her own village.

She had been gone so long that she had forgotten her own people. She watched as they went about their daily work. The women at the cooking fires were telling stories, the children were out gathering water from the stream and firewood, and the men were out hunting. The young woman was filled with loneliness for her own people; she started feeling homesick. When her husband, Morning Star, returned, he could see what she had done. He said, "What you have done is not good. You have pulled up the sacred turnip and now you must return to your own people." He was very sad to have to let her go. He called for all the buffalo hides to be brought to him and he made a long rawhide rope. He tied it around his young wife and carefully lowered her back down to earth.

On earth she lived again with her own people. She shared the wisdom she had learned during her time in the Sky Country. This wisdom became the foundation for the Sun Dance—*Oka 'ni*. She brought with her the rawhide rope to tie the poles of the Sun Dance Lodge, and also the sacred turnip—the *Maas*.

To this day, it is an honoured woman who vows to have the next Sun Dance Lodge.

The girl who married the Morning Star taught the people many things: sacred songs and prayers, the pipe ceremony, the blessing of face painting, special ceremonies to bless babies, and how to use the sweat lodge to cleanse the body and mind. To this day, women gather to give thanks at the Sun Dance for the safety of their loved ones and for those who have returned home safely from hunting. And so the sacred teachings of the Sun Dance continue to this day, and we remember the girl who married the Morning Star—*Aa pii so woh sa*.

AUTHOR'S NOTE

The Girl Who Married the Morning Star is a story of the Blood-Kainai people of southern Alberta. This story was developed through oral storytelling by Mary Hays, *Ii' yin ni maa kii*—She Who Captures and Louis Soop, *Pii tai kiih tsi pii mi'*—Spotted Eagle. Mary and Louis tell the story in tandem, in English and in Blackfoot. The beauty of the combination of the two languages and the two voices brings this moving story to life. It is a story of how love and lost love bring the sacred traditions of the Sun Dance to earth from the Sky Country.

The Story of the Thumb-Sucker

A German Tale

by Catherine Melnyk

There once was a little boy named Konrad, who lived with his mother just outside the bustling town of *Bergstadt.* Konrad was like most little boys. He liked to play in the dirt and wrestle, but Konrad also liked to suck his thumbs. This made him known to all the other children as the *Daumenlutscher* or 'thumb-sucker'! Konrad would suck his thumbs all year round, even when he was helping his mother with *Hausarbeiten!* She begged him not to suck his thumbs, but 'plop' they would go into his mouth while he rested from shovelling the snow, weeding the garden, and especially while watching television. Often Konrad's mother would pull Konrad's thumb out of his mouth and say, *"Hör auf am Daumen zu lutschen!"* but Konrad thought he was clever, and when he would take one thumb out, 'plop,' there went the other thumb.

Now Konrad's mother was a superstitious woman. She was worried about her son growing up to be a man who still sucked his thumb. More importantly, though, she was concerned that if Konrad was not a good boy and did not stop sucking his thumbs, the Slicer would come and remove his two thumbs in a most terrible fashion. She had heard this from her own grandmother.

One day, Konrad's mother asked him to come to the garden to help her dig potatoes and carry them to the kitchen so she could make *Kartoffelsalat*. Konrad came, as asked, though he dragged his feet. Oh, what a garden it was! There were lettuce, tomatoes, cucumbers, carrots and peas, and like most gardens, in which sons don't help out often, there were lots of *Pusteblumen*. Instead of helping dig up potatoes, Konrad's mother told him he could pick weeds. Konrad complained in between sucking his thumb, "Ah, (slurp) *nein,* Mama, I (slurp) hate *Unkraut!*" Konrad did not want to pick weeds, and he thought this was the worst job imaginable, so he sat down in the black dirt and continued to suck his thumb in protest.

Konrad's mother sternly said, "Konrad, do not suck your thumb or the Slicer will come to get you! He likes to hide in the weeds. If we pick the weeds, he will have nowhere to live and will go find another family to bother. We must pick the weeds if you want to keep those thumbs!" But Konrad continued to suck his thumb and looked at the clouds instead of listening to his mother.

Meanwhile, the Slicer was hiding amongst the weeds and was watching little Konrad, thinking to himself how very much he would like to add a new set of thumbs to his collection. The Slicer wanted to collect as many thumbs as possible. The Slicer was in constant competition with his brother, Cutter, who did not take thumbs, but instead chopped locks of beautiful hair off the heads of little girls who did not brush their hair. Cutter had already collected golden, black, brown, and red locks that summer, while the Slicer had claimed no fingers at all. Slicer eyed up Konrad, and thought that this little

boy should be watched more closely to make sure that he truly deserved to lose his *Daumen.*

The next day, Konrad's mother was washing dishes and asked Konrad to help her dry the pots and pans, but Konrad was too busy sucking his thumb to hear her request for help. All Konrad could hear was the "Suck! Slurp! Slop!" of his thumb in his mouth. Konrad's mother said, *"Du sollst nicht so oft an deinen Daumen lutschen Konrad!* Konrad, don't suck on your thumb so much! The Slicer will see you and come claim your thumbs as a trophy! Also on your hands are germs, and you should not put your thumbs in your mouth unless you want to get sick."

"Get sick?" Konrad thought, "Hmmm..." Getting sick did not sound so bad to Konrad because he could miss school and stay at home and suck his thumbs. Earlier in the school year, the other kids on his school bus and in his class made fun of him when they learned that he sucked his thumbs. They called him a 'big baby' and a *'Daumenlutscher,'* and now Konrad did not like to go to school anymore. With the idea that he would not have to go to school if he got sick, Konrad smiled and continued to suck his thumb. Through the kitchen window, the Slicer saw that Konrad ignored his mother's request to help dry the dishes, and thought to himself, "If I see little Konrad not help his mother one more time, his thumbs will be mine!"

Later in the week, Konrad's mother decided to go into town to sell the vegetables from her garden. Konrad's mother asked Konrad, "Will you help me?" but Konrad was not a sweet little boy anymore, and all he wanted to do was suck his thumb, so he ignored his mother again.

Konrad's mother sighed and said, "Konrad, I am leaving to go to town. If you keep sucking your thumbs, the Slicer will come and take them from you! Be good, and if you will not come to town with me, please dust for me while I am gone!" And of course, as soon as Konrad's mother left to town, 'plop,' in went his thumb. The moment Konrad put his thumb back into his mouth, there was a loud 'crack,' and right in front of him, to Konrad's *Überraschung,* the Slicer appeared! Without haste, Slicer crouched down in front of Konrad and said, "Now I go Klipp and Klapp with my scissors, and off go your thumbs with my big sharp shears!"

Konrad screamed in panic, "Hey! Ow! Help!" and the Slicer said, "You should have helped your mother when she asked you to, and you should have listened to her warnings about me!"

Konrad pleaded with the Slicer to give him back his thumbs, and exclaimed, "Please, Slicer, I know I have been naughty and I should have listened to my mother! Please! What can I do to get my thumbs back?"

Slicer was surprised by Konrad's plea for help, and although Slicer was known for collecting and keeping little children's thumbs, he also was occasionally known to give them back if, and only if, the child showed remorse. Slicer sized up Konrad as he continued to beg for his fingers back.

"Bitte!" Konrad cried, "My mother warned me about you and I did not listen. What can I do to make up for my ignorance?"

Slicer thought for a moment, and then replied to Konrad, "It just so happens that I do, only in special circumstances, return thumbs … so I propose a deal

for you. If you help the other little boys and girls around your school and tell them not to suck their thumbs and fingers, I will give you back your thumbs in two years' time."

"Two … years?" Konrad whispered.

"Yes," replied the Slicer, "two years, one year for each thumb. If you follow my orders, I will be back and return to you what I have cut off," and then there was a loud crack and Slicer was gone.

Konrad was in shock, as he was left thumbless, crying and alone. After Konrad's tears had stopped, he considered what Slicer had told him to do in order to get his thumbs back. While waiting for his mother to come back from town, he decided that he would follow the Slicer's order, and stop other kids from sucking their thumbs.

When Konrad's mother returned, Konrad was waiting at the door for her. She saw that Konrad was standing there without his thumbs, and ran up to Konrad weeping. "Oh Konrad, the Slicer came, *es tut mir so leid!* What are you going to do, now that you have no thumbs?"

Konrad told his mother that if he was good, and taught the other boys and girls not to suck their thumbs, that the Slicer would be back in two years' time, and that he might be able to get his thumbs back.

Konrad's mother thought this was an acceptable plan and so they began to wait for the two years to pass until the Slicer's return. During those two years Konrad dutifully helped his mother with chores, as best he could since he was missing thumbs, and he taught the other children not to suck their thumbs.

And so, in two years' time, to the date exactly, Konrad's mother again planned to go into town to sell her vegetables and leave Konrad to face the Slicer alone. She was surprised when Konrad offered to help her and said, "But Konrad, today is the day the Slicer promised to return with your thumbs! If you come into town with me, you will miss the Slicer and not get your thumbs back."

Konrad replied, "I would rather make sure my mother got to town and back again safe and sound, and help her sell the vegetables, than get my thumbs back."

The Slicer who had been hiding behind the cauliflower in the vegetable basket jumped out and said, "Konrad, you have truly learned your lesson!" Then the Slicer chanted:

> *With a pinch and a stitch and a sew*
> *Konrad shall have no more woe*
> *The thumbs you lost shall be returned*
> *Since you have shown me what you learned!*

A loud 'crack' occurred and Konrad's mother exclaimed, *"Konrad, du hast deine Daumen wieder zurück bekommen!"*

The Slicer then spoke again and told Konrad, "As a reminder for you and for all the little boys and girls, your thumbs will always be smaller than the rest of your fingers because they were not attached to you when you were growing up to be a good son!" With a final 'crack,' the Slicer was gone. This though, was not the end of the thumb-sucker collector, and the Slicer continued to collect thumbs throughout the country, but he was also known to return the thumbs if the children showed that they deserved to get their thumbs back. Konrad and his mother were so pleased that he got his thumbs back that they jumped for joy, and then headed into town to show that Konrad had got his thumbs back after all.

AUTHOR'S NOTE

The Story of the Thumb-Sucker was one that my second generation German-Canadian friends and family told me. The version of *The Thumb-Sucker* that my living family members and peers could first recall hearing and reading was from a collection of short stories within *Der Struwwelpeter* (Shaggy-Peter) (1845) by Heinrich Hoffman. Further, in the 'original,' Konrad does not have his thumbs returned to him—this is never an option. Konrad is only portrayed as a naughty boy, who unfortunately does not listen to his mother and in the end, is physically punished with the removal of his thumbs. I decided to alter the story, so that Konrad is able to learn a lesson and have an opportunity to earn his thumbs back. The moral of the story then changes from one that is meant to warn children that their actions could produce dire consequences, to a story that instead demonstrates the moral that there is reward for changing one's behaviour in a positive direction.

The Woodpecker and the Cunning Fox

A Tale from Afghanistan
by Marghalara Rashid

Once upon a time, there was a hungry and cunning fox who decided to enter a nearby village. In spite of knowing the cost of going into the village, he made his way to the hen coop of the closest *bazgar* and snuck in through a small hole between the door and the post. The *bazgar*, who had grown smarter over the years, had made a very high perch for the hens. The fox tried jumping as high as he could, and just as he thought he had got hold of one of the hens, he lost his grip and fell down. The fox ended up in a vat of white paint and all the hens laughed at him. He could feel his paw pounding, as it had hit the side of the container.

Now, he was not only hungry, but his self-esteem was down and his paw was extremely hurt. He picked up a stick and started to walk on his two legs to keep pressure off his hurt paw, and got away as fast as he could before the *bazgar* woke up.

As the fox rushed off, a fowl called out, "*Kaka, Kaka chere rawan yey*? Uncle, Uncle where are you going?"

"*Chare na yam rawan.* I am not going anywhere," replied the irritated fox.

"Are you going to *Hajj*, wearing your white outfit, and carrying a *lakana*?" asked the fowl.

Assessing the entire situation quickly, the cunning fox replied, "Yes, I am going to *Hajj*."

"*Kaka, Kaka ma la zan sara na biya yey*? Uncle, Uncle, will you not take me with you?" the fowl asked.

"*Wagey kege, tagey kege, bya ba ma ta jzarey*. You will get hungry and thirsty and then you will cry," said the fox.

"No, no, I will not get hungry and I will not get thirsty, nor will I cry," said the fowl.

"Jump onto my back then," said the fox. The fowl instantly obeyed the fox and jumped onto his back.

A little further on, they met a duck who, on seeing the fowl on the fox's back, immediately wanted to know where they were going.

"I am going to *Hajj*," said the fox.

"*Kaka, Kaka ma la zan sara na biya yey*? Uncle, Uncle, will you not take me with you?" asked the duck.

"*Wagey kege, tagey kege, bya ba ma ta jzarey*. You will get hungry and thirsty and then you will cry," said the fox.

"No, no, I will not get hungry and I will not get thirsty, nor will I cry," said the duck.

"Jump onto my back then," said the fox, and the duck jumped on the fox's back. With the duck and the fowl on his back, the fox tried to get home quickly. Walking on only two legs, while carrying the duck and the fowl, was very difficult for the fox. As he rushed to reach his den, a woodpecker called out, "I am going to *Hajj*, too; may I join you?"

"*Kaka, Kaka ma ham la zan sara na biya yey*? Uncle, Uncle, will you not take me with you as well?" the woodpecker asked.

"*Wagey kege, tagey kege, bya ba ma ta jzarey*. You will get hungry and thirsty and then you will cry," the fox responded.

"No, no, I will not get hungry and I will not get thirsty, nor will I cry," said the woodpecker.

"Jump onto my back then," said the fox.

Taking all three birds, the cunning fox finally arrived at his den. The birds were all a little astonished at this stop, but they accepted the fox's justification of having to rest a bit and make further arrangements for the long journey to the *Hajj*. In the meantime, the fox made a decision about how and which one to eat first.

Soon the fowl, who was extremely eager about his journey, started barging and boasting. The fox swooped in and swallowed him in one gulp. He explained to the astounded birds that it was essential, because they could not continue on such a long journey with someone so troublesome and annoying. The duck, who had sat quietly all day, suddenly wanted to take a quick dip in the lake, and asked the fox for permission to do so. The fox gobbled her too, saying that someone who cannot make it one day without water cannot travel such a long distance.

The intelligent woodpecker, who had carefully judged the whole situation told the fox, "You must be dehydrated, uncle; let us go and I will get you some *shede* to drink."

They went back toward the village. When the woodpecker saw girls taking *shede* to the market, he pretended to be hurt and jumped a few steps in front of them. The girls, seeing this gorgeous bird clearly hurt, put down their *shede* and started following the bird. The bird led them as far away from the *shede* as it could, so that the fox could drink the *shede*. The bird flew back to the selfish fox and told him, "Uncle, you relax, while I go and get some more *shede* for you."

The fox happily accepted his offer and instantly fell asleep. Meanwhile, the smart woodpecker went and found a *bazgar* who was working in his fields. He played that he was injured and directed the *bazgar* to the sleeping fox. The *bazgar* trapped the fox. Thus, the clever woodpecker took revenge for the death of his beloved friends.

AUTHOR'S NOTE

The story originates from Afghan culture and is a popular story among the Pashtun tribe. The moral of the tale is that deceiving someone in order to fulfil one's own greed is an unjust action, for which the offender will sooner or later be punished. I heard this story from my grandmother when I was five years old. The story is well accepted in the southernmost parts of Afghanistan, where Pashto is spoken. While *Hajj* is a pilgrimage that Muslims undertake, in some stories, it is also used in a humorous way to make fun of those whose actions are not religiously inclined.

GLOSSARY

bazgar—farmer

Hajj—pilgrimage

lakana—cane

shede—milk

The Figs and the Golden Whistle

A French Folktale
by Melissa Morelli Lacroix

A long time ago, when there were still dukes and counts and barons spread throughout the land, there lived a rich marquis in a *château* in Auvergne, that green expanse of rolling hills and sleeping volcanoes in the centre of France. This marquis liked fine things: fine robes, fine wine and fine figs—sweet, delicious figs. He ate figs for breakfast, lunch and dinner, and then before bed, he tucked a fig under his pillow to help him have sweet dreams at night. One night, however, something troubled the marquis so much that even the sweetest fig beneath his pillow would not allow him to rest. He rolled to his right, he turned to his left, then finally he sat up in bed. "I think it is time for our daughter to marry," he announced to his wife.

"Se marier?" the marquise asked, waking from her sleep with a start. "But whom shall she marry?"

"Exactement! Qui?" the marquis wondered as he chewed on his fig. "That is what has me tossing and turning this night."

"Perhaps our daughter has an idea; after all, many suitors have come to see her."

"Too many," complained the marquis. "She will never be able to choose."

"We should have a contest then," suggested the marquise.

The marquis ran his tongue over his fig-sweetened lips as he considered this idea. *"Oui!"* he cried suddenly. "We shall have a contest—a fig contest." The marquis spoke as he wrote out a declaration right there in his bed, "To the man who brings me the sweetest figs, I will accord my daughter's hand."

News of the marquis' contest spread across the valleys and over the hills to the farthest corner of Auvergne where a peasant lived with his three sons on a small parcel of land next to a tiny fig grove. When the peasant heard of the proclamation, he made his way to the fig grove and carefully selected the finest figs, and placed them in a covered basket that he handed to his first son. *"Vas-y, fiston.* Take these to the marquis," he said, "and soon you will be the heir to the richest man in Auvergne. "

The son took the basket and made his way toward the marquis' castle. On the way, he came across an old woman, who stopped him and asked, "What have you there in your basket, *jeune homme?"*

The peasant's son was worried the woman would want to eat his figs, so he answered, "Nothing but rabbit droppings, *Madame."*

The old woman's forehead wrinkled with surprise, and she replied, "How odd. But may all go well with you, just the same." And the two parted ways.

When the peasant's son arrived at the marquis' castle, he bowed before the wealthy man and humbly presented him with his basket. The marquis eagerly took it and opened it without delay. *"Des crottes de lapins!"* he roared and threw the basket back at the peasant's son. "Take this man away!" And the peasant's first son was thrown out of the castle, never to be given a chance to see the young bride.

When he returned home, the peasant's first son recounted what happened. His father shook his head with disappointment, but he had another son who could win the hand of the marquis' daughter if only he did not make the same mistake as his brother had made. The peasant returned to the fig grove and carefully selected the finest figs, and placed them in a covered basket that he handed to his second son. *"Vas-y, fiston.* Take these to the marquis," he said, "and soon you will be the heir to the richest man in Auvergne."

The second son took the basket and made his way toward the marquis' castle. On the way, he came across an old woman—the same old woman who had stopped his brother. "What have you there in your basket, *jeune homme?"* she asked.

Like his brother, the peasant's second son was worried the woman would want to eat his figs, so he answered, "Nothing but pebbles, *Madame."*

The old woman's forehead wrinkled with surprise, and she replied, "How odd. But may all go well with you, just the same." And the two parted ways.

When the peasant's second son arrived at the marquis' castle, he bowed before the wealthy man and humbly presented him with his basket. The marquis eagerly took it and opened it without delay. *"Des cailloux!"* he roared and threw the basket back at the peasant's son. "Take this man away!" And the peasant's second son was thrown out of the castle, never to be given a chance to see the young bride.

When he returned home, the peasant's second son recounted what happened. His father shook his head with disappointment, but he had yet another son who could win the hand of the marquis' daughter if only he did not make the same mistakes as his brothers. The peasant once again returned to the fig grove and carefully

selected the finest figs, and placed them in a covered basket that he handed to his third son. *"Vas-y, fiston.* Take these to the marquis," he said, "and soon you will be the heir to the richest man in Auvergne."

The third son took the basket and made his way toward the marquis' castle. On the way, he came across an old woman—the same old woman who had stopped his brothers. "What have you there in your basket, *jeune homme?"* she asked.

"Only the finest figs in all of Auvergne, *Madame,"* the third son replied. "Would you care for one?"

The old woman's forehead wrinkled in surprise, "Indeed," she said, and gratefully accepted the fig the young man offered. *"C'est délicieux,"* she praised as she smacked her lips together in delight.

"Merci," the third son replied. "Would you care for another fig?"

The old woman nodded, *"Oh, oui!"* And she greedily stretched out her hand.

"Please, have another fig," the third son offered again and again, until all but one fig were gone.

"Oh là là!" exclaimed the old woman. "I have eaten all of your figs."

The third son surveyed his basket. *"Mais non,* there is one left, and that is all I need." He recovered the basket and bid the old woman good-bye.

"Mais attendez," she called after him. "I must pay you for the figs."

"Oh no," the third son protested. "I can't ask for that."

"You are not asking," the old woman replied as she reached below her cape and produced something that she pressed into the third son's hand, "I insist."

The peasant's son took what the old woman had given him and studied it—a golden whistle. He did not know what he would do with such an item, but he graciously accepted it. The old woman smiled. *"Gardez-le bien,"* she advised. "Keep it safe—it may serve you well one day." And with that, the two parted ways.

When the peasant's third son arrived at the marquis' castle, he bowed before the wealthy man and humbly presented him with his basket. The marquis eagerly took it and opened it without delay. *"Oh là là,"* he marvelled, as he gazed upon a plump-full basket of the largest figs he had ever seen. "These look mighty fine." He plucked a fig from the top of the pile and plopped it into his mouth. "Mmm," he sounded with delight. "Mmm … this is the most delicious fig I have ever eaten. *Vous gagnez!"*

The people assembled in the room began to cheer, but the marquis' head servant leaned close to the fig-lover's ear. "Sir," he whispered, "he is the son of a peasant."

"Un paysan?" The marquis coughed and choked on his fig. When he composed himself he made an announcement so to save himself from the disgrace of having a peasant marry his daughter. "You have won, *jeune homme,* but before you can have the hand of my daughter, you must fulfill another task." The assembly quieted and listened to the marquis. "For twenty days and twenty nights, you shall guard twenty hares in the north field. If you do not lose a single hare during that time, I will accord you my daughter's hand."

"Très bien, Monsieur," the peasant's third son agreed, and he followed the marquis' men to the north field, where twenty hares were set loose and promptly ran off in every direction. The peasant's third son chased after them over the grass and through the bluffs, but to no avail—all of the hares were lost. Discouraged, the young man fell to the ground and cried. After a time, he searched in his pocket for a handkerchief to wipe his eyes, and he came across the golden whistle that the old woman had given him in exchange for his figs. Hoping to cheer himself, the peasant's third son brought the whistle to his lips and

blew it. Instantly, the twenty hares bounded their way back to the young man, and he understood the meaning of the gift he had been given.

For two weeks, the peasant's third son allowed the hares to roam the north field during the day, and then he blew the golden whistle to call them back for the night. They always came—not one was ever lost. The marquis heard of this and became enraged. "I cannot have a peasant marry my daughter! I must do something." So he disguised himself as a traveller and made his way to the north field. The peasant's third son saw him approach and immediately recognized the marquis' noble gait, but he did not let on. *"Monsieur,"* the marquis said, "I see you have many hares. May I buy one for my supper?"

"Oh no," the peasant's son replied. *"Ils ne sont pas à vendre."*

"S'il vous plaît," the marquis begged, "my children are very hungry."

"D'accord," the peasant's son agreed, "if you can pay the price."

"Anything," the marquis agreed.

"I will give you a hare, if you allow me to kick you three times," replied the peasant's son.

The marquis reddened with anger, for he suspected that the peasant's son knew that it was he; but he agreed, for he did not want his daughter to marry such a poor man. The kicks were given, and the marquis went away with a hare in a canvas bag. As he neared his castle, however, the hare became agitated, and thrashed about the bag with such force that the marquis was unable to hold

onto it. The bag fell from his hands, and the hare escaped, running back to the north field, where the peasant's third son sat blowing his golden whistle.

As the peasant's third son continued on with his successful hare herding, the marquis' daughter became nervous about her impending marriage. She decided, therefore, to go have a look at her future groom. She disguised herself as a traveller and made her way to the north field. The peasant's son saw her approach and immediately recognized her noble gait and suspected that she was the young bride, but he did not let on. *"Monsieur,"* the marquis' daughter said, "I see you have many hares. May I buy one for my supper?"

"Oh no," the peasant's son replied. *"Ils ne sont pas à vendre."*

"S'il vous plaît," the daughter begged, "my children are very hungry."

"D'accord," the peasant's son agreed, "if you can pay the price."

"Anything," the marquis' daughter agreed.

"I will give you a hare, if you allow me to kiss you three times," the peasant's son replied.

The young woman reddened with shyness, but she agreed, for she found him handsome and intelligent. The kisses were given, and the marquis' daughter went away with a hare in a canvas bag and a pounding heart in her chest. When she reached the edge of the field, she released the hare and encouraged him, "Go now, run back to your master." And the hare did just that, for at that very moment the peasant's third son sat blowing his golden whistle.

Finally, after twenty days and twenty nights, many lords and ladies filled the marquis' grand hall in order to watch the peasant's third son once again bow before the marquis. *"Monsieur,"* the young man said, "I have successfully completed your task."

"So I've heard," the marquis replied. "But there is one more thing you must do in order to win my daughter's hand." The marquis threw a canvas bag before the peasant's third son and said with a smirk, "You must fill this bag with the truth."

The peasant's third son knew that what the marquis asked was impossible, nonetheless he leaned forward to pick up the bag. As he did so, he whispered to the marquis, *"Monsieur,* I will happily do as you wish, but in order to do so I will have to tell all of the people assembled here that you bought a hare in exchange for three kicks from a peasant and that you were unable to keep that hare, one single hare, for twenty minutes, while I, a peasant's son, was able to keep twenty hares for twenty days and twenty nights."

The marquis reddened, and without hesitation he announced, *"Et voilà!* The bag is filled! Toll the wedding bells!"

AUTHOR'S NOTE

The Figs and the Golden Whistle (known in French as *Panier de figues et sifflet d'or*) is a traditional tale from the central region of France called Auvergne, but there is a similar story about figs and a bugle in Italian folklore as well. The dates of origin of the stories are unknown. I first heard this story as an adult, and soon thereafter I began telling it to my children, who have both Auvergnant and Italian ancestry. *The Figs and the Golden Whistle* is an entertaining story about class distinctions and using wits to overcome prejudice.

GLOSSARY

c'est délicieux—it's delicious

château—castle

d'accord—all right

et voilà—and here we are

exactement! qui?—exactly! who?

gardez-le bien—keep it safe

ils ne sont pas à vendre—they are not for sale

jeune homme—young man

madame—madam

mais attendez—but wait

mais non—but no

merci—thank you

oh là là—oh wow

oui—yes

se marier—to marry

s'il vous plaît—please

très bien—very well

un paysan—a peasant

vas-y, fiston—go, son

vous gagnez—you win

the Twelve Forest Folk

A Czechoslovakian Tale
by Jennifer Maruno

Long ago, in the foothills of the Bohemian Forest, a woman lived with two girls. Maruška, her gentle, pretty niece, kept the cottage clean, cooked and tended the garden. Holena, her harsh and ugly daughter, sat by the window and sewed. But Maruška did not complain. She bore her burden of labour, her aunt's scolding and her cousin's unreasonable demands with a smile.

One winter morning, Holena called out from her bed. "I cannot get up," she said. "I feel I will not live without the taste of an apple."

Her mother rushed to her side. "Maruška will find you one," she promised.

"But, apples do not grow in the snow," Maruška said.

"Vzitsi," her aunt shouted, as she pushed Maruška out the door into the wind and snow.

Maruška remembered a pair of ancient fruit trees on the mountain, beyond *Král smrku,* the King of the spruces. She made her way along the trail, through the deep snow, hoping to find just one withered apple.

As she approached, Maruška saw a light in the distance.

A large fire burned in the middle of the circle of stones. Twelve forest folk sat on the stones that surrounded it.

Maruška, feeling the cold, went to the man on the highest stone. His hair, beard, and brows were as white as the snow. "Please, sir," she asked. "May I warm myself at your fire?"

The great, white man nodded. Then he asked, "Why have you come to the top of the mountain on such a cold day?"

Maruška glanced at the bare branches of the trees with disappointment. "I am searching for an apple," she said.

"Apples don't grow in the winter," the man said.

"It is for my ailing cousin," Maruška told him.

The man rose from his stone. "Září," he said to the man dressed in autumn leaves, "take my seat."

As soon as the man sat down, the fire burned bright gold. The snow around the apple trees melted, revealing ferns and ivy. Red apples dangled from the very top branches.

"Shake the tree once," Září commanded.

Maruška shook the tree and an apple tumbled down. She thanked the people with all her heart and ran home.

Holena grabbed the apple and bit into it. "This is the most delicious apple I have ever tasted," she said.

"Where are the rest?" asked her aunt. "Did you eat them on the way home?"

"There was only one," Maruška said. "The man told me I could shake the tree just once."

"Then you are a fool," her aunt said. "You will not get even a taste."

The next day Holena flopped into a chair. "I cannot stand any longer," she said. "I feel I will never walk again without the taste of a strawberry."

"Strawberries do not grow in the snow," Maruška said. But it did not matter. Her aunt turned her out the door.

Maruška, remembering the warm earth beneath the apple trees, made her way back up the mountain. This time the journey was colder and longer. At last she saw the light of the great fire. The great, white man was once again seated upon the highest stone, surrounded by forest folk.

"Please, kind sir," Maruška asked. "May I warm myself by your fire?"

He nodded. "Why have you come to the top of the mountain again?"

Maruška glanced at the snow beneath the trees. "I am searching for strawberries."

"Strawberries don't grow in the winter," the old man said.

"The apple gave my cousin enough strength to get out of bed," Maruška said, lowering her eyes to the ground. She was not happy to pretend there was real illness.

The man rose from the stone. He walked to the woman in green leaves, seated across from him. "Červen," he said, "take my seat."

As soon as the woman sat down, the fire burned bright yellow. The snow on the trees melted. Green leaves covered their branches. Strawberry plants filled the ground.

"Gather them quickly," Červen commanded.

Maruška filled her apron pocket. She thanked the people with all her heart, curtseyed and ran all the way home.

The scent of strawberries filled the air as Holena and her mother took them from her.

"These are the most delicious strawberries I have ever tasted," her aunt said as she ate them.

"Why are there not more?" asked Holena. "Did you eat them on the way home?"

"A woman told me to gather quickly," Maruška protested. "I took only a pocketful."

"You should have taken more," the aunt shouted, "no matter what! You will not have one."

The next day, Holena picked up her embroidery. Looking at the purple thread, she sighed. "How I long for the scent of violets," she said. "I can no longer breathe this stale air of winter."

Maruška reached for her coat, but this time her aunt stopped her. "I will go," she said, picking up her basket. "Why just gather violets where there are strawberries and apples as well?"

The mother, wearing Maruška's coat over her own, struggled through the deep snow to the top of the mountain. Seeing the fire, she put her basket down, stepped into the circle and warmed her hands.

"Who do you wish to help this time?" the man asked, recognizing the coat.

"Myself," the aunt said as she turned her back to him. "Mind your own business."

The man stood in anger and the sky grew dark. Thick snow fell, making the fire sizzle. An icy wind blasted through the forest.

Holena waited for her mother by the window. As the sky darkened, she put on her coat. She wrapped Maruška's shawl over her coat and made her way to the mountaintop.

Seeing the fire, she approached it. She spied her mother's empty basket on a stone outside the circle. "What have you done?" she shouted at the people sitting in a circle. "Why have you robbed my mother of her apples and strawberries?"

The white man waved his hand. The shawl fluttered away and the fire went out.

Maruška waited and worried, but having no warm clothing, she couldn't venture out.

In the spring, Maruška returned to the mountaintop. There was no fire and the forest folk were gone. She found her shawl and coat on two small stones outside the circle. Her basket sat on a carpet of sweet-smelling violets. As Maruška filled the basket with violets, she wondered where her aunt and her cousin had gone.

Maruška lived in the cottage, tending and caring for it as usual. A young farmer soon came to share a long, contented life with her in the cottage.

Author's Note

While walking an Ontario forest path, my friend, Georgina, suggested we keep an eye out for the twelve forest folk. Intrigued, I asked her what she meant. We sat together on a large rock as she told me a favourite tale of her Czechoslovakian childhood.

This ancient tale of Slavic peasants and herdsmen was first translated into English from French in 1896. Maruška's story, mixed with an unusual touch of retribution, reminded me in part of the time-honoured tale of Cinderella, in which a hard-working girl's kindness helps to overcome the cruelties of a wicked stepmother and stepsisters. It also shows how those with hearts of stone often turn to stone because of their own actions.

the Flying Head

Based on a Woodlands Native Story and Personal Experience
by Antoinette Botsford

"Antoinette!" scolded *Gran'mamère*. "Don't go into the *forêt*—the woods—alone when it is getting dark."

When I was just a little girl, we were camping at Fish Lake. Our camp was right near the lake—we pretty much had it to ourselves—there were no public washrooms, or running water spigots or anything like that back then. It was real camping.

We caught, salted and dried fish. Then we went berry picking, and finished off the hot afternoon with a swim in the lake. This bath was the only kind of cleaning we had during the wonderful weeks of 'fish camp.'

My favourite thing to do on these summer trips was to slip away from everyone and watch for creatures of the night. I'd wonder at the owls, which, with the softest flutter of velvet wings, would sweep upon their prey. I'd spy on the sleek and sneaky weasels, as they slipped out of their hiding places to explore the possibilities of night, when life really began for them. However much *Gran'mamère* might scold, the magic of the forest at night would call to me and I couldn't stop myself; I'd just slip away, captivated by the sounds and shapes and mysteries of shadows playing in the growing darkness.

One night, I stayed away far too long and wandered so far from camp that I was beyond the reach of anyone's voice who might be calling me from our campsite. It wasn't until I saw a lantern coming toward me in the darkness that I realized I was really in for it this time.

When I got back to the campsite, *Gran'mamère* took me aside. Her wrinkles looked deeper, especially the furrows between her black eyebrows. She really had been worried.

"Antoinette, écoute! On à dit qu'il y'à une tête volante dans

le forêt. Listen, Antoinette. Word is out that there's a flying head in the forest."

"A flying head!" I gasped. *"Gran'mamère, qu'est que c'est une tête volante?* What is a flying head?" Chills crept up and down my spine.

"It is too terrible for me to speak about, but *très dangereuse.* Please say nothing to the others about this. They will have *cauchemars.*" Her mouth became a hard little line bisecting the deep creases that ran from her nose to her jaw, and I knew better than to ask for more information. For the rest of fish camp, I did not stray from the campsite after dusk. Even when I went to the latrine, I took somebody with me.

All the while I kept asking myself, *"Qu'est-ce que c'est une tête volante? Qu'est-ce que c'est une tête volante?* What is a flying head?"

We returned home to the farm, and after Mass, I breathlessly ran over to my aunt's house. Aunt Antonia was also my godmother. *Grande'tante* Antonia had grown up in rural Quebec, and spoke a flavourful patois—in this case, a mixture of French interspersed with some words of indigenous origin—common to the people from that region in the late 19th century. I rushed over to her house. A widow for many years, my godmother was always ready to tell me a story or give me a cookie. She was tiny and dark, except for her hair, which was like pure snow, and she could often be found tending her rose garden. She would tell me more about flying heads, I felt certain.

"Tante Antonia," I called out.

"Chere-chouette, little owl, what is on your mind?" my aunt asked.

Before long, the story tumbled out of me. *"S'il vous plâit, ma grande'tante— qu'est-ce que c'est une tête volante?* You must tell me. What is a flying head?"

My aunt put down her knitting and looked at me over the top of her glasses. "What are you talking about, my dear? How can there be such a thing?"

"There is!" I insisted. *"Gran'mamère m'a dit …"*

"Well," said my aunt, thoughtfully. "I thought the world was finished with such things. But if my very own brother's wife says there is such a thing, why then it must be true, even nowadays." She shuddered.

"But what IS one?" I begged, thrilled to be at the threshold of a good story.

Before she would tell me, she made me promise not to say anything about it to my cousins. "It will give them nightmares for no good reason, for if they do not go alone into the *forêt* at dusk there will be no problems with flying heads."

"But me," I cajoled, "I like to go into the forest at dusk; you'd better tell me."

"Yes," she sighed. *"Il faut …"*

And so she started her story.

* * *

A long time ago, before even the French people came to Canada, one of our First Nations ancestors was alone in the village with her baby. Her people were away at fish camp, but she had stayed behind to keep an eye on things.

The people were away longer than expected and there wasn't much food in the camp, so the young woman decided to go pick some berries. She put her baby on the cradleboard on her back, took her baskets, and went into the forest and started picking. Oh, she picked and picked, filling her little baskets and pouring them into the big basket. The berries were perfect. She picked for the whole day, with her baby on her back. Then, just about dusk, she heard a high scream coming from the air, not like any bird she'd ever heard.

She looked up. High in the sky, coming right at her, was a HEAD! A huge head, with streaming red hair and a wide mouth, coming right at her!

She dropped the berries, headed toward the nearest tree, and leapt into its branches, climbing quickly to where the head would not see her and the baby.

The head saw her big basket of berries there on the ground. It opened its mouth wide and slurrrrrrrrrrped them up in one big gulp. It took them all inside. Then his long nose began twitching. It twitched in the direction in which the mother and baby had gone. Sliding along on its own slobber, it followed the scent until it arrived at the place where the woman had jumped into a tree.

There the scent stopped. The head followed its nose around and around the tree, snuffling in disappointment, trying unsuccessfully to track the woman.

High up in the tree—a pine tree, by the way—the mother looked down on the terrible head—the head that had just finished eating ALL her day's work and was now, she was sure, ready to devour her and her baby.

Her heart pounded. She hoped the baby would not cry.

As for the baby, he was being good, and quiet. But he was curious, as babies always are. He saw a pinecone. He reached out for it, knocking it off the branch. It went tumbling down to the ground, rolling right past the head, which turned around, followed it, and ate it up with one huge CRUNCH.

While the head was chomping on the pinecone and looking the other way, the young woman hurried down the tree and headed for the thorny berry bushes. She figured that if she dropped to her belly and slithered on the ground, the head would have a hard time following her. The bushes would catch its hair, and it would get stuck. She could hurry back to her lodge. That was the plan—it came in a flash, faster than words can say.

The head heard her and saw her disappearing into the bushes. It finished the pinecone and went right after her. But the woman had arms and legs, and could crawl quickly, and even though the thorns caught her hair and her clothing, she paid no attention.

But the head's long red hair got stuck in the branches, and with only its nose and nimble tongue to help, it would take a long time to get free.

The woman reached her village. *"Awiija!"* she cried out, "Anyone here?" There was no answer. She rushed to her lodge, hurried inside, piled up every box and heavy thing against the entrance, and built a fire. She sat beside that fire, nursing her baby, and realized that she was also very hungry.

There was nothing to eat in the lodge but chestnuts, so she put some of these into the fire.

Meanwhile, the head was struggling to follow the woman. Much of its hair was caught in the bushes. It was half-scalped now, and madder than ever. When it got to the village it could smell the chestnuts cooking and could see smoke coming from the woman's lodge. It rolled up to her door and threw itself against the blockade with a huge bump.

But it wasn't enough to break down the barrier, so it decided to go to the top of the house and look through the smoke hole. With a big WHOOSH, it got to the roof and looked down through the smoke. It saw the lady raking what looked like coals from the fire—and—what? Eating them!

In a gravelly voice, the head said, "I didn't know you could eat *akakanzhe*. Very well, I will have these, and then I will eat the *anishinabekwe* and have her *dakobinaawaswan* for dessert!" The head stretched its mouth wide open and went straight down to the fire and sucked up all the glowing coals in one big slurp.

Not delicious—the fire coals burned the head's mouth terribly!

With a horrible shriek, the head surged upwards through the smoke hole—high, high into the sky, heading north in a blaze of flame.

Shaking, the young mother sat by the fire with her baby. She would not leave the lodge until her people came back the next day. When she told them what had happened, they said that the night before they had seen a ball of fire high in the sky, heading toward the land of eternal snows. Some thought it was a shooting star. Some said it was an evil spirit from the Northern Lights. But they never saw it again, not ever. People still talk about that clever and brave young woman who saved her child from the flying head.

* * *

The story was over. *Tante* Antonia looked at me with her black eyes twinkling. "So, *Cherie,*" she said, "now you know what is a *tête volante*. And until now, they say that was the end of the *têtes*. But you never know. They have a powerful *magique.* If *ma belle soeur* says they come back, then maybe they will. So don't go in the woods by yourself when it is getting dark, *hein?*"

Suffice to say, I stayed out of the woods at dusk. Even though I suspected it was a ploy between my *Gran'mamère* and *Grande'tante* to keep me in line, I wasn't sure. I'm still not.

AUTHOR'S NOTE

Antoinette first heard this story when she was about 10 years old (ca. 1950) through her mother's description of a camping trip on Mount St. Helens in Washington state in the 1930s. In this retelling, Antoinette imagines herself as a combination of her mother and her child self, turning to those who first told the story, and enriching it with her own memories of family elders. There is a similar story of Iroquois origin. These stories celebrate the bravery of women, and the power of a mother's love.

The Monkey and the Crocodiles

A Sri Lankan Tale
by Henry Victor

There was a huge *kulam,* a lake, on the outskirts of a village named *Periya Kulam,* which means 'big lake,' in an eastern province of Sri Lanka. In the murky waters of that lake, a crocodile named Thuttan lived with his wife, Thutti. Hardly anyone living in *Periya Kulam* ever went to swim or to fish in that lake. The villagers kept away from the lake. They feared the crocodiles, Thuttan and Thutti, as they were known to have dragged and drowned many goats, sheep, and cattle that had come to the lake to drink.

By the side of the lake there was a tall and massive *naval,* that is, a purple tree. The tree was known by that name because of the purple colour of its fruit. On that tree was a playful, friendly *kuranku,* a monkey named Mithuran. Mithuran loved the *naval* fruit. It was like cherries. Soon the *naval* season came. Mithuran always looked forward to this season. But the villagers believed ghosts haunted this *naval* tree. And, therefore, no one ever dared to go near the tree to pick its fleshy fruits, leaving Mithuran to have all of them.

One day, Thuttan, the male crocodile, swam near the *naval* tree and asked Mithuran, *"Athu enna sappidukirai?*

69

What is that you are eating? *Ennakum russi parka ondru tharu-vaya?* Can you give me also one to taste?" Mithuran, friendly and very generous by nature, enthusiastically plucked some *naval* fruits and dropped them into the lake. Thuttan ate them and liked them very much. Every day, from that day on, Mithuran gave *naval* fruits to his new crocodile friend.

One day, Thuttan took a few *naval* fruits to Thutti, his wife. Thutti liked them very much. She asked Thuttan, *"Intha palankkal unakku enkirunthu kiddaithanna?"* From where do you get these sweet fruits?"

At this point, Thuttan spoke about his new monkey friend, Mithuran, who had been giving him the delicious fruits daily. Thutti then said, "You say that the monkey on the tree eats lots of these sweet fruits. I am sure his liver will be sweeter. I would like to eat the monkey's liver." Thuttan was shocked at his wife's desire. He told his wife that Mithuran was a good monkey and a very helpful friend. To take Mithuran's liver out, one would have to kill him. And it is not fair to repay evil for good.

Thutti, the evil crocodile wife, was in no mood to listen to the 'preaching of her husband,' and she began to cry in rage. At this point, Thuttan promised his wife that he would somehow bring his friend's liver on the next day.

Early next morning, as usual, Thuttan swam to the *naval* tree and laid himself silently, but with a long face. When Mithuran saw his friend was sad, he inquired about the cause of his sorrow. Thuttan told the monkey, "My wife is very sad because you are not visiting our house. And I am sad because I have not introduced my best friend to my wife. Today she woke up very early and has made lots of special sweets for you. Will you please come to my house, that my wife and I can also repay you for all your goodness?"

Mithuran replied, *"Aum,* of course, I would like to visit your home. But you live in the middle of the lake where the water is very deep and I do not know how to swim. I can only climb a tree and leap from branch to branch; in water, I will drown to my death."

In his heart, Thuttan thought that he was close to satisfying his wife's distorted desire. Hence, he became very confident. He calmly told his monkey friend, "That is no problem at all. Why am I here? Friends must help each other. I will help you in that adventure. You can sit on my back and I will carefully carry you to my home. And you will not get wet in the water."

Mithuran agreed and quickly leapt on to the crocodile's back. When the friends were in the middle of the lake, where the water was very deep, the crocodile laughed out loud and revealed to his friend, who was now comfortably seated on his back, "Actually my wife wants to taste your liver. She believes the liver of the monkey who eats so many sweet *naval* fruits ought to be sweeter still. That is why I am taking you. Today we will both eat your liver and enjoy our sweet, sweet supper."

Mithuran couldn't believe his ears. Could friends behave in such an evil manner? But he was poised and clever and he calmly replied to Thuttan, who was bent on fulfilling his wife's wicked desire, "Oh, Thuttan, you should have told me this earlier. My liver got wet in yesterday's rain. So I have taken it out and hung on the tree to dry."

When Thuttan heard his friend, he told the monkey, "If that is the case, I will take you back to the shore, to the *naval* tree. You can climb up the tree and bring back your liver. If I take you home without your liver, my wife, in her anger, will go for mine." And even before the monkey agreed, Thuttan began to swim speedily to the shore.

As soon as they reached the shore, Mithuran jumped off, climbed the tree and pelted a pebble at the crocodile. He yelled, "Hey, *thee-ya mada-yaa*, hey, evil fool, so generously did I give you fruits! And still you wanted to kill me! From now on I will offer you no more fruits. This marks the end of our relationship." And Thuttan, truly saddened, swam back to his wife.

AUTHOR'S NOTE

This folktale, which originates perhaps from the ancient collection called *Panchatantra,* and is related to other collections, such as the *Aesop's Fables* and the *Buddhist Jataka* tales, is a very popular folktale told with many variations to children all over the world. It is now also part of reading for elementary school children in Sri Lanka and other countries in South Asia. It is believed that some of these stories were first written down in Sanskrit around two millennia ago. The purpose of the folktale is not merely to be entertaining; it is also a subtle tool with which to convey morals. The moral of this tale is cultivating the skill of remaining cool even in moments of adversity. From the monkey's cool-headedness, one may also learn and affirm the superiority of wit and diplomacy over brute force. Others may suggest that this tale also teaches that greed can lead to the loss of an important friendship, just as the steady supply of tasty fruits is lost. In the Tamil language, Thuttan and Thutti, the names of the male and female crocodiles, refer to male and female 'evil persons' respectively. Mithuran, the name of the monkey, means 'friend.'

More Than a Caterpillar

A MEXICAN TALE
BY DANIELLE LAMB

Not long ago in *el Valle,* a host of flowers flourished. Among them was Mariposa Lily. The Mariposa Lily was unique, not only because it looked like a butterfly from the periphery, but also because it attracted caterpillars from throughout *el Valle* who produced beautiful *rebozos,* traditional Mexican woven shawls. The head caterpillar had a vision to make Mariposa Lily the most flourishing *rebozo* fabricator in *el Valle.* Now this was no small task for the head caterpillar, as there were many ornate lilies throughout the valley producing *rebozos.* Yet the head caterpillar pondered, "How can I make the biggest, brightest, and most beautiful *rebozos* in *el Valle?*"

After much contemplation, the head caterpillar concluded that in order to fulfill this task she needed to bring together a group of caterpillars. She put out notices to neighbouring vines, trying to recruit the best caterpillars. Days passed—even weeks. And finally the head caterpillar found four fresh and young caterpillars. Now these were no ordinary caterpillars, but special caterpillars—coloured caterpillars—each of whom had their own unique colour. Each of the caterpillars was named according to her colour: Rojita, the red caterpillar; Moradita, the purple caterpillar; Verdita, the green caterpillar; and, Azulita, the blue caterpillar.

Daily, the caterpillars worked together using their different strengths and colours to create picturesque *rebozos,* and soon the Mariposa Lily *rebozos* were being recognized throughout *el Valle,* and into the forests and surrounding mountains. Not only were their works being praised, but many noticed the friendship that was developing between the four industrious caterpillars. The head caterpillar's wish had come true, but here is the odd thing: while the relationship among the coloured caterpillars blossomed, their relationship with the head caterpillar began to disintegrate. The head caterpillar began to chastise the four. Despite the amazing *rebozos* that they produced, the head caterpillar disapproved of the way the elements were woven together. Breathing heavily through her side and stomach, the head caterpillar shouted, "Verdita, you need to weave those tighter!" So Verdita wove her green strands tighter.

"Azulita, you need to add more blue," she demanded. And Azulita added more blue.

"Moradita and Rojita, your *rebozos* need to be bigger!" she said, and her voice got louder.

And so Moradita and Rojita spent longer hours weaving to make the *rebozos* bigger. Together the four caterpillars made the *rebozos* tighter, brighter and bigger.

But still, the head caterpillar always found something to complain about; nothing could please her. Over time this miserly head caterpillar began to change form. Her brownish colour became more and more dull, and an unwelcoming odour began to emit from her body

amarillo—yellow

azul—blue

con—with

el Valle—the valley

mariposa—butterfly

morado—purple

naranja—orange

negro—black

rebozo—a woven scarf or shawl that can be used to carry children or products to market. Some feel that the *rebozo,* made by weaving fabrics together, is a metaphor for the Mexican people as decedents of the indigenous and Spanish people.

rojo—red

rosa—pink

verde—green

74

as she squirmed along the stem, and the shrill sound of her commands got harsher. The air felt heavy and burdensome. It was horrid, and the caterpillars grew concerned, but none of them wanted to leave the place: they stayed at Mariposa Lily because they looked forward to seeing each other every morning, and because they knew the *rebozos* they were creating could only be produced by their intricate weavings of *azul, verde, rojo* and *morado.*

Daily, the trials and tribulations continued and the songs that once danced throughout the stems when the coloured caterpillars were at the peak of production began to sound like a piercing cacophony. Soon, one by one, the colourful caterpillars began to lose their radiant colours, and they began to contemplate their work at Mariposa Lily. Not only was production down, but even the friendship seemed to suffer. They all needed to escape, but to where? The other stems and vines in *el Valle* were not in need of weavers.

One evening, after a long conversation, the four coloured caterpillars agreed that despite the awful conditions that they had endured, and the illness of the head caterpillar, the friendship that bound them together outshone the dark days at Mariposa Lily. Then suddenly, amidst their chatting, something began to happen. One by one, the caterpillars' segments began to tighten, and soon all four of them were paralyzed. Azulita, Moradita, Verdita and Rojita could not move. What was happening? The four friends could not move, and worse, they could not weave. They were terrified. They watched in horror as the smelly old caterpillar invited a new caterpillar to the Marisposa Lily and the manufacture of the beautiful *rebozos* continued without them!

Days passed, even weeks, and then one by one the cocoons that had paralyzed each of the coloured caterpillars began to shatter, and one by one, the coloured caterpillars began to stretch out. The little tubular round segments that had once made up their bodies were beginning to change shape. As they emerged from the cocoons, it was as if Nature had carefully hand-painted a new colour on their wings: Moradita *con negro;* Azulita *con rosa;* Verdita *con amarillo;* and Rojita *con naranja.*

It was only then that these four friends, once caterpillars, began to realize that they had always been designed to blossom. They were never meant to be limited to their weaving. They were more than caterpillars. They were always meant to be butterflies—beautiful butterflies—and now they were ready to fly. Together the four friends took to the air and a new song filled *el Valle.*

AUTHOR'S NOTE

This story is inspired by different Mexican folktales about the caterpillar and the butterfly, *el gusano y el mariposa,* that date back to the time of the Aztecs. When I was living in Mexico, I heard a story about a caterpillar that struggled to figure out what its purpose was. Even though the caterpillar works hard and weaves beautiful creations, it must learn to be patient. The moral of the story is to always try your best because in the end you do not know what your reward will be. For the caterpillars of this story, their hard work, and the unity with which they worked, paid off when they realized that they were meant to be butterflies.

Shirin and Farhad

A Persian Folktale ·
by Marghalara Rashid

Once upon a time, there lived a poor man named Farhad. Farhad was a sturdy and brave man, who was a *sang tarash,* a stone carver. One fine day, Farhad was enjoying his leisure, taking a lazy walk along a river. Suddenly, he saw a beautiful gold thread floating in the water. Farhad wondered what it could be. He approached the water and quickly got the thread. He realized that it was not a thread, but a long beautiful hair. He thought, if this hair is so gorgeous and fragile, how beautiful would be the maiden to whom it belongs? He asked many people around the village if they knew any lady with gold hair, but unfortunately, no one identified the hair.

One day, when he was taking a walk again, he saw a beautiful lady with long gold hair and he fell in love instantly. As time passed, Farhad's feelings grew for the beautiful maiden and he wanted to marry her. But the people of the village told him that it was not possible for a poor man like him to get married to her, as she was the *shah*'s daughter, Shirin.

The *shah*, who cared for his daughter and loved her dearly, did not wish for Shirin to marry someone who was poor and not of royal blood. The *shah* heard that

Shirin had been furtively meeting Farhad. The *shah* got worried for the princess, and the future of his kingdom, as he had no other children. He decided to conduct a meeting in his court to discuss this issue with his *viziers*. All the *viziers* proposed different and evil ideas to get rid of Farhad. They debated for a long time, after which one *vizier* proposed that they should send Farhad to *Koi Kaf*.

"Send him to *Koi Kaf* your majesty," said the *vizier*, "and ask him to free the caged nightingale whose cage has been hanging in a well near the enchanted palace of the dragon."

"And then what?" asked the *shah*.

"Think, my majesty, think! The dragon will be killed, my lord, and *Koi Kaf* will be yours," said the clever *vizier*.

"Yes, but what about my daughter? She will be Farhad's," said the *shah*.

The evil *vizier* laughed. "We will kill him and that will be his end."

"I cannot kill him—my daughter will be hurt, and she will hate me for the rest of my life. I am old and I do not want to die with that guilt," said the *shah*.

The other *vizier* who was sitting next to the king said, "We all know that this is an impossible job and Farhad will not be able to reach those mountains alive, let alone free the bird."

"Yes, yes, he is right," said the other *viziers*. Finally, the *shah* sent word to Farhad that if he freed the bird, the *shah* would give him his daughter's hand in marriage.

Farhad agreed and said to the *shah's khabar rasan*, "Please go tell your *shah* that with all my heart and soul, I, Farhad, the lover of his beloved daughter, Shirin, accept his demand and give my word that I will go to *Koi Kaf* and free the bird."

Immediately, Farhad started preparing, and the night before he left, he went to the palace to meet Shirin and say, *"Allah hafiz,"* to her.

The next morning, Farhad set out for his long journey with the hope that he would soon return to his beloved Shirin. He did not see any human for many days. As days passed, he got tired; there seemed to be no end to the long road. After many days, he reached a place where he saw a small cottage. As he went closer he saw an old man sitting outside the cottage. The old man was very kind-hearted and hospitable. Farhad spent the night with the old man; after a long time he slept well. In the morning when he was leaving the old man's house, the old man told him that on his way, he would encounter an old woman.

"If you go and hug her from behind without letting her know, and kiss her hands without fear and with *ehtaram*, with respect, she will be the world's most kind and affectionate woman you have ever met," said the old man.

"I will do as you say and respect her like my own mother," said Farhad.

"Son, if you please her, she will give you important clues that will help you reach *Koi Kaf*."

Farhad kissed the old man's hands, showed his appreciation for all his help and hospitality, and continued with his journey.

As he was climbing the hill, he saw a woman with her back towards him; she was sitting and praying. He approached the old woman very quietly. As he hugged her, she opened her eyes and embraced him back, as if she had just seen her own son after a long, long time. Farhad kissed her hand and paid his respects to her. The old woman told Farhad exactly where the nightingale was. She gave him a bunch of her own hair and said,

"Son, when you need help, burn my hair. When I smell my hair in the air I will know that you need *komak*, help."

When Farhad reached *Koi Kaf*, he felt happy and nervous. Finally, after many days, he found the well and it was time for him to call the old woman for help. It seemed impossible, but as he burnt the hair, the old woman appeared and on seeing her, he was delighted.

"Mother," he said, "I will go down into the well before the sun rises and the dragon wakes up."

He gave her a rope and said, "You hang on to one end of the rope and I will take down the other end. If I don't move up the rope before the sun rises, you may leave, as it will be a sign that I am dead." But before it was morning, Farhad came up with the cage in his hand. As he freed the bird there was a thunderstorm and lightning all over *Koi Kaf.* The dragon died as soon as the bird was freed.

Farhad went back to the *shah,* but his *viziers* came up with another task. They told Farhad that the *shah* was not happy that he took such a long time to perform the simple task of freeing the bird. Farhad was disappointed, but he could not say anything for the sake of his beloved. He had no choice, and quietly and helplessly he agreed to the second task.

In the second task, he was asked to dig a canal that was forty miles long. The vicinity where the canal was to be dug was rocky and hilly. It looked like an impossible task. However, Farhad did not back down from it. He began excavating and cutting rocks. Farhad worked day and night to get the task done; it took him a very long time to finish this job. Shirin occasionally went to visit Farhad. She observed him working. Then she rode back to the palace. Finally, Farhad dug the canal and accomplished the task.

However, he was assigned one more task by the *shah.* He was required to dig a well in a rocky place. Farhad set to work and had the well halfway dug. Now the *shah* feared that Farhad would complete this task as well, and that he would have to allow Farhad to marry Shirin. Some of the king's *viziers* suggested a dirty trick. They said that an old woman should go to Farhad and tell him that Shirin had died. The king agreed to the suggestion.

An old lady was sent to the place where Farhad was working. She wept and told Farhad that his princess was no more in this world. This broke Farhad's heart, and he died because of grief. When Shirin heard about Farhad's death, she hurried to the place where his body lay. After watching the dead body of her beloved, her heart was broken too and she died beside Farhad's grave. According to people, the bodies of Farhad and Shirin were put in the same tomb, and they lie there together forever, and the story of their love is still told around the world.

AUTHOR'S NOTE

The story of *Shirin and Farhad* is very popular around the Middle East, as well as in South Asia, and is an important part of Persian culture. As it has travelled through various cultures, it has taken elements from other folktales as well. The version here is the one that my grandmother used to tell me when I was a child. As I grew up, I realized that she mixed many folktales as she told this story to me in Persian. Folklore from around the world has various stories, such as *Laila and Majnun,* or *Romeo and Juliet,* which rejoice in true love. Although a bit gloomy, this story celebrates true love, and the perseverance of Farhad amidst all the hardships.

The Sun, the Cold and the Wind

A LITHUANIAN FOLKTALE
BY JURATE MOTIEJUNAITE

One day—a long, long, long time ago—Saulė, the sun, Šaltis, the cold, and Vėjas, the wind, were walking down the road, arguing.

Saulė said, *"Aš stipriausia iš visų!* I am stronger than both of you!"

Šaltis responded, *"Ne, aš stipriausias.* No, I am stronger!"

Vėjas did not want to give up, *"Aš stipresnis už jus abu.* That's not true! I am stronger than both of you!"

They all thought that it would be much easier for the strongest one to live in the world. But how could they decide which one of them was the strongest?

On their way, Saulė, Šaltis and Vėjas met a man. The man, politely, took off his hat and bowed to them in greeting. Then he walked on.

Before the man had walked too far on, the three travellers called him back. "Tell us," they asked, "which one of us did you bow to?"

The man thought very carefully. He did not know how to answer, as he did not want to offend any of the three. If he offended Saulė, the sun—she could make him too hot. If he offended Šaltis, the cold—she could freeze him. If he offended Vėjas, the wind—Vėjas could dry the Earth. Who deserved the most respect? Who was the most helpful to the man?

Finally, the man decided that it would be best to say that he had bowed to Vėjas, the wind. After all, he thought, Vėjas would be the most helpful. If Saulė heated too much, Vėjas would blow from the north and cool everything off. If Šaltis made it too cold, the southern Vėjas would warm everything up. So the man said, "I bowed to Vėjas."

Saulė did not like the man's response, so she threatened, "All your life, you will regret your decision that the wind is the most important!"

Vėjas, however, reassured the man, "Do not fear Saulė or Šaltis. If they want to harm you, all you need to do is think about me."

As soon as the summer came, Saulė, the sun, decided to teach the man a lesson. She took all her strength and heated everything up. The man was so hot that he didn't know what to do—he couldn't find a cool place outside or inside the house. He tried cooling off in the water, but he couldn't sit in the water all day.

Then suddenly, he remembered Vėjas and said, "Oh, if only Vėjas blew, it wouldn't be so hot!"

With those words, Vėjas blew from the north, and it cooled off right away. The man could do his work, and Saulė had to admit that Vėjas was stronger than she was, and more helpful to the man than she was.

When the winter came, Šaltis, the cold, decided to teach the man a lesson. She brought on such freezing cold that the man could not take his fur coat off, not even inside his house. The man again remembered Vėjas and said, "Oh, if only there was some southern wind, it would not be as cold."

Then Vėjas blew from the south, and it started warming up; the man could go on with his work. Then Šaltis realized that Vėjas was stronger, and more helpful to the man.

The man walked to the forest to get some wood for his fire. On his way, he again met Saulė, Šaltis, and Vėjas. The man looked at them all and said, "The one who is the strongest does not take pride in the strength. Only good deeds and helpfulness can show who has most strength."

Real strength is determined by good actions.

AUTHOR'S NOTE

This story is typical of Lithuanian tales about nature. I first heard it when I was a child, at a school in Lithuania. Although it is difficult to identify the approximate date of the story's origin, it probably dates from before the 15th century. Lithuania was officially Christianized toward the end of the 15th century, but folk stories representing pre-Christian religion continued to be told, and were recorded by writers toward the end of the 19th century. Pre-Christian religion in the Baltic region (which includes Lithuania) was based on a belief in the interdependence between human beings and nature. The natural forces in the pagan Baltic religions were personified; thus, stories exist about an angry Sun, a benevolent Wind, a lonely Moon or a beautiful Earth. The role of such stories is to explain the natural phenomena, as well as to outline the proper behaviour between human beings and nature. This particular story aims to exemplify the different powers the sun, the cold, and the wind have on human beings, and to teach the importance of good deeds. In other words, the man chooses Wind because of Wind's positive actions and helpfulness.

the Flow of Water

A Sikh Legend from India
by Dalbir Sehmby

Rushing horses stormed the field, sleek arrows darkened the sky, and shimmering steel swords clashed! Soldiers battled like thunder and lightning ripping through the hot Indian sky. The army of the Emperor was at war with the army of the 10th Guru of the Sikhs. However, on the dusty battlefield, within the cruel dangers of war, in 1705, there was a Sikh, Bhai Kanhayya Ji, who walked without any weapon.

Instead of armour, a shield, and a sword, Bhai Kanhayya Ji wore simple clothes with a white flag of peace tied to the left side of his belt, and he carried a heavy *mashk*, a leather bag filled with cool drinking *paani*, or water. As Sikh soldiers fell to their wounds, gasping for help, Bhai Kanhayya Ji rushed to their comfort, serving refreshing water to their parched mouths. Most peculiarly, Bhai Kanhayya Ji also gave water to wounded enemy soldiers.

Frustrated by his actions, a few Sikh soldiers grabbed Bhai Kanhayya Ji and took him to the Guru, voicing their complaints, "This Sikh has gone crazy. We commend him for bringing us water, but we must also condemn him. While we have been trying to defeat the enemy, he has been giving water to them!

He's bringing back their energy and bringing more trouble for us."

Having heard the accusers, the Guru asked Bhai Kanhayya Ji to speak for his actions.

Bhai Kanhayya Ji humbly spoke, "I give water to wounded soldiers with no concern for which side they are fighting on, because when I look around on the battlefield, all I see are human beings. I look around and see you everywhere. I see that your divine light pervades all, dear Guru."

The Guru stood up and declared, "Bhai Kanhayya Ji, for such actions, I must give you …"

Anticipating a severe punishment, the accusers grinned.

"… I must give you …"

The great warrior poet Guru Gobind Singh reached for something. Was it a *talwar*, a sword? Would he punish Bhai Kanhayya Ji for his foolishness? Would he whip the hands of this traitor? Would he cast him out full of shame for ignorance?

"… I must give you these gifts to further help your wonderful *sewa*."

The accusers were shocked. The Guru handed Bhai Kanhayya Ji some medicine and wraps to cure the wounds of soldiers on both sides of the battlefield.

AUTHOR'S NOTE

As my late father Swaran Singh Sehmby explained when he told this story to me, this story promotes humanitarian values of kindness and selfless service to all. The message of this story lies in Bhai Kanhayya Ji's (1648–1718) gift of water. Water is a symbol of life. The gift of water is precious because it can save lives. Water also symbolizes some of the main tenets of Sikh faith. The same water of life flows through all of us. If all humanity is one, then why should we discriminate on the basis of race, faith or ethnicity? As water flows through different rivers, there are several paths to enlightenment. Bhai Kanhayya Ji left behind a special movement in Sikhism, the 'Sewa Panth,' akin in spirit to the Red Cross. *Sewa*, or selfless service to all humanity and volunteerism, is the central aspect of the Sikh way of life. It is a way of active meditation through community service. Sikhism was started by Guru Nanak (1469). In Sikhism, *Guru* is a special reverential title given to its ten spiritual teachers. Guru Gobind Singh (1708) was the 10th and last Sikh Guru. The title of the 11th spiritual leader is given to the Guru Granth Sahib, the central Sikh treatise. It was composed by a number of the Sikh Gurus but also includes spiritual writings from non-Sikh spiritual leaders.

The Story of Dingxiang

A Tale from China
by Xie Wenjuan

A long, long time ago, there was a city in China called Hangzhou. At that time, Hangzhou was the most beautiful and the most prosperous city in China. Among the richest business families, there was a Zhang family. The Zhang family had only one child; his name was Wennan. Wennan was married to a beautiful girl named Dingxiang. They had led a happy life since being married three years ago, but the only sad thing was that they did not have any children.

One day, when Dingxiang was out, a neighbour, Miaoxiang, came to visit Wennan. Miaoxiang was once a close girlfriend of Dingxiang, but recently she had become more and more jealous of Dingxiang's wealthy life. Seizing the chance when Dingxiang was not at home, she said to Wennan, "Why do you still want Dingxiang as a wife since she cannot give birth to even one child in three years? You should break up with her and find a new wife."

Wennan did not answer her at that time, but he did take her words to heart. After pondering on it for a few days, he finally decided to go to see a *Suanming xiansheng,* a fortune-teller. He found a fortune teller on the street

and asked him whether his wife Dingxiang would have a good fortune. The street fortune teller closed his eyes, counted his fingers several times (yes, that's the way the fortune teller told the fortune, by counting his own fingers), and answered, "Yes." Then Wennan asked whether the neighbour girl Miaoxiang had a good fortune. "No," he counted his fingers a few times again and replied, "She will bring disaster to her family." But eager to divorce Dingxiang and marry Miaoxiang, Wennan did not believe the fortune-teller's words; further, he paid the fortune teller a good amount of money and bribed him to lie about the fortunes of Dingxiang and Miaoxiang if he were asked the same questions by others.

When Wennan came back, he told his father, Old Zhang, that Dingxiang must have a bad fortune since she could not bear children for the family, and he wanted to marry Miaoxiang instead, who was more beautiful and younger. Old Zhang did not believe his words at first and asked him to bring a fortune teller so he could verify. Having been paid by Wennan, this time the fortune teller told a lie. He replied to Old Zhang that Dingxiang truly had a bad fortune, while Miaoxiang was the fortune-favoured one. Upon this, the Zhang family finally decided to divorce Dingxiang, the kind wife, and send her to her parents' home.

Knowing nothing of her husband's plot, Dingxiang, the innocent wife, was shocked at this notice. She asked her husband Wennan, "Why do you divorce me? Is it because I haven't cared for you?"

Wennan answered, "No."

Dingxiang asked again, "Is it because I haven't loved you enough?"

Wennan again said, "No."

Again Dingxiang asked, "Is it because I haven't been nice to your family?"

Wennan replied, "No. Not because of any of these. I have to send you home because you cannot bear me children." Hearing this, Dingxiang was heartbroken, yet she could not say a word for herself because this was unfortunately true. So, she was sent off from the Zhang's house.

The day when Dingxiang had to leave, her ex-husband Wennan said to her, "You can take with you anything you want from the house."

She replied, "I will take some clothes and a horse for the journey home, and nothing more." The Zhang family then gave her what she asked for.

Embarrassed to return to her parents' home, for in those days a divorced daughter was a humiliation for her family, Dingxiang talked to the horse, "Dear horse, if you have sympathy for me, please be my matchmaker and take me to my man." Immediately, as if it understood her words, the horse took her to the road. The horse did not stop for a second until sunset.

At sunset, Dingxiang found herself before a very old thatched cottage at the foot of a high mountain. An old woman came out of the cottage at the clop of the horse. Dingxiang asked the old woman, "Old mother (because in ancient China, this is a polite way to speak to an elderly woman), do you have a son?"

"Yes, I do have one son. He is cutting firewood in the mountain. But why do you ask?" she replied. Cutting branches from trees in the mountains and selling them as firewood was the livelihood for many poor families then.

Dingxiang smiled and said, "Because I come here to be his wife, old mother." The old woman was very happy to see such a beautiful woman willing to marry her son, especially when she could not find a wife for him, because they were so poor. She invited Dingxiang into the cottage at once.

Soon, her son, whose name was Li, came home with two loads of heavy firewood on his shoulder. Just like his mother, Li could not believe such a beautiful and well-bred lady would be willing to become his wife. He thought himself not a match for her; his clothes were shabby, his hair disarrayed, and his face black and dirty. However, Dingxiang said nothing about it and did not mind sleeping on the floor with a worn-out quilt.

The next morning, Li got up very early to sharpen his axe, as he usually did before heading to the mountain to cut branches again. Dingxiang also got up early to make breakfast. And when she saw the stone on which Li was sharpening his axe, she asked Li, "Dear husband, where did you get the stone from?"

Li replied, "From the other side of the mountain. There are lots of stones like this."

Then Dingxiang said to him, "Do not tell others about the stones, for they are very precious stones and worth one thousand *liang* gold each."

Dingxiang then asked Li to take the stone to the *qianzhuang*, the money bank, where he could exchange the gold stone for money. Li went to the *qianzhuang* in town instead of cutting wood. Soon he came back with one thousand *liang* gold, just as Dingxiang said. The family was overjoyed, especially Li and his mother, for they had never seen so much money before.

On the second day, Dingxiang asked Li to have a haircut, shave his beard, take a bath, and buy some new clothes in town, since they now could afford it. Gladly Li went to the market stores. When he came back, Dingxiang and his mother could hardly recognize him; he was, in fact, a very handsome young man. Later, they sold many stones that they got from the other side of the mountain and built a large house in town with the wealth they made. One year later, Dingxiang gave birth to a son for Li's family, and they lived very happily.

However, the Zhang family was not so fortunate. Soon after driving Dingxiang out from the house, Wennan married Miaoxiang, the jealous neighbour. But it happened that at the wedding night's celebration, the *bianpao,* firecrackers, accidentally jumped into the haystack in the yard, eventually causing a fire so severe it burned down the entire house and killed everyone in the house except Wennan, who was now blinded. So, on his wedding night, Wennan lost everything and became a blind beggar. He began to beg from one place to another, and knew neither where he was nor what day it was.

Glossary

baozi—steamed bread pies; traditional Chinese food

bianpao—firecrackers, often lit at celebrations and festivals

liang—the unit of money used in ancient China. One *liang* is 50 grams.

miantiao—Chinese noodle; traditional Chinese food

qianzhuang—the private bank in the old times of China. *qian* means money, and *zhuang* means house; *qianzhuang* literally means money-house.

suanming xiansheng—a Chinese fortune-teller

xinfang luocheng—the completion of a new house. It is the old custom in China to have a big banquet when one family has built a new house, and often rich families will give out food for beggars.

One day, Wennan travelled to a new city and heard that there was one rich family giving out food on the street to celebrate *xinfang luocheng,* the completion of a new house. He was carried by the crowd of beggars to the front door of the new house. The family was, in fact, the Li family and this was their second new house.

"Please give me some food! Please give me some food!" Wennan begged in the noisy crowd. Dingxiang, who was giving out the food, found the voice very familiar, and when she looked closely at the beggar before her, she recognized that it was her ex-husband, Wennan, though he did not recognize her because of his blindness. Dingxiang then invited Wennan into the house and cooked him some *miantiao,* noodles. Because he was so hungry, Wennan gulped the food without even thanking the hostess. Then he started crying, and said to Dingxiang that the taste of the noodles was very much like his ex-wife's cooking.

The next day, the Li family was giving out the charity meals again. Because they were very generous, there was an extremely long line of beggars. Among the beggars, Wennan was the last one in the line. It happened that the Li family ran out of the food when it was Wennan's turn. When Dingxiang saw all this inside the house, she asked the servant to invite Wennan in again and cooked ten *baozi,* steamed bread pies, for him. When Wennan got the pies, he sold nine of them and left only one for himself to eat. At his first bite, he felt something hard inside the pie. He thought it was a bone and cursed about how the rich people never put good meat but bones in the pies. He spat it out angrily, but when he spat it out, other beggars cried out that it was in fact a piece of gold. Not long after that, Wennan heard that the rich lady of the new house was called Dingxiang. Then Wennan understood that it was Dingxiang that cooked him noodles and hid the gold in the pies. He cried, "What a fool am I!" He then left the city in remorse and no one knew where he went.

Author's Note

This is a story my grandma told me when I was nine, or younger. I vaguely remember there was a good wife humiliated by her husband who was rewarded with gold stones for her integrity in the end. The world, in which the good and the poor are rewarded with good fortunes, in which good deeds bring good results eventually—the eternal theme and dream in folk imagination—was very appealing to me. Later, I tried in vain to look up the story in story collections, so I asked my grandma to retell the story to me after many years. She recalled that this was a story she remembered from a local opera in Southern China when she was a child. The version recorded here is created, therefore, not only by the dreams of the old, good, simple Chinese folk hearts, but also by the memory gaps of the grandma, and the cultural re-imagination of the granddaughter.

Frida's Flute

A JEWISH FOLKTALE
BY SHOSHANA LITMAN

Frida concocted the best games of any kid on her block. She could juggle jelly beans and run rings around her Momma and Poppa in an argument. What Frida loved to do most was play the flute. She played her little wooden flute in the kitchen, the living room, the backyard, upstairs, downstairs—you name it—there she'd play it. Frida's flute made the most wonderful sounds in the world. Ask Frida any question and she would give you the most amazing answer, but not with words. Frida answered questions with her flute. When her parents wanted to know where she went, Frida played a song to answer them. When her friends wanted to know how to play a game that only she knew how to play, Frida composed a tune to answer them. The tunes she produced were fabulous and fun. When Frida played her flute, the wind and trees kept time.

Frida loved to play flute most of all outside under her favourite tree, an old gnarly maple covered with soft green moss. Frida nestled herself into a curved spot in the old tree's trunk. Then she'd play and play her flute all day.

What she did not love was homework. Now Frida was clever and could do many things. She could dance, do somersaults, snap her fingers, whistle and sing. But try as she might, Frida could not learn to read.

Her parents tried to help. Her teachers tried to help. Even the wisest teacher of all, Rabbi Eliezer the Wise, tried to help. They played *aleph bet*—the Hebrew alphabet—games with Frida, made up *aleph bet* rhymes, sang *aleph bet* songs with her ...

> *Aleph, bet, vet,*
> *gimel, dalet, hey,*
> *vav, zayin, chet, tet,*
> *yud, kaf, chaf,*
> *lamed, mem, nun,*
> *samech, ayin, pey, fey,*
> *tzaddi, kuf, resh,*
> *shin, sin, tav.*

They even turned the letters of the *aleph bet* into chocolate for Frida to eat. The letters tasted delicious and Frida gobbled up every one. Still, she could not learn to read.

After a while, everyone gave up.

Now it so happened at this time, that a terrible cloud covered the earth. This cloud was so thick that you could scoop it with a spoon. The sun could not get through the grey cloud to warm the earth. People's prayers could not get through the heavy cloud to reach Heaven.

Things got worse and worse. Plants stopped growing. People stopped smiling. Even the birds stopped singing.

Eliezer, the Wise, who had read every good book that had ever been written, thought he knew why. He sensed that bad deeds and empty prayers had made that cloud, which was not letting the prayers go up. Eliezer, who was wiser than wise, came up with a plan. He called everyone into the town's tiny synagogue, the place where they met to pray.

It was dark and cold in the old, dusty hall because the sun did not shine through the windows. Eliezer told jokes to make everyone laugh, but no one smiled even though he told very funny ones. Then Eliezer explained what they must do.

"My sweetest friends! Please pray with all your heart, all your soul and all your might. If we do this, then maybe, just maybe, we can break through this terrible cloud together."

Everyone concentrated very hard. They scrunched up their faces. They thought about sunshine and singing birds and laughing children. They prayed every prayer in their prayer books with all their hearts, souls and might.

Nothing worked. The sky remained thick and dark. No one smiled. No birds sang.

Frida stood beside her Momma, wrapped in a golden shawl. Frida concentrated harder than anyone. Frida felt the big cloud rolling around in her head. That nasty cloud made her forget all the prayers she knew by heart. Frida wanted to help but she did not know how.

Then Frida remembered her flute. She thought about how good she felt playing her flute under the mossy maple in her backyard. Thinking about her flute made her want to play it. She pulled her little wooden flute from her pocket and began to play.

Frida played her flute like she never had before … as if she were nestled in her tree and all the birds on the earth sang with her.

Suddenly, the air in the old synagogue lightened. A gentle wind wafted into the room. Frida felt a fresh breeze touch her face. She ran to a window to see outside.

"Look!" Frida cried. "The cloud is gone."

Frida could see everyone's prayers rush to Heaven, following the music of her flute.

Frida felt so good. She put her flute back into her pocket. She hugged her Momma. She hugged her Poppa. She hugged her friends. She hugged Eliezer the Wise.

Then Frida took out a prayer book. The prayers in her prayer book started to make sense. Very slowly at first, then faster and faster, she began to read.

"Look," Frida explained to her Momma. "See how the letters work together to make words?"

Nothing stood in her way now. When Frida spoke the words out loud, they sounded like music. The sweetest music she had ever heard.

After that awesome day, Frida played her flute as much as, if not more than, before. She still juggled jelly beans, ran rings around her Momma and Poppa in arguments, and concocted the best games of any kid on her block. Only now she also read and wrote stories like this one, just for you.

AUTHOR'S NOTE

Frida's Flute is based on a story told in Eastern Europe by the Baal Shem Tov (1698–1760), a great leader also known as Rabbi Israel ben Eliezer, about an illiterate boy whose heartfelt prayers reached Heaven when no one else's could. There are several versions of this story. *Frida's Flute* reminds us that there are many ways to contribute to society, as well as many forms of literacy. The chocolate letters are reminiscent of an old Jewish custom of putting honey on the first letters a child learns to read to encourage them to associate learning with sweetness. It is my hope that this story will also provide encouragement to those who struggle to learn to read. I first heard this story from an accomplished Jewish storyteller, Helen Mintz, of Vancouver, British Columbia, in the early 1990s at the Victoria Jewish Community Centre.

the Farmer and His Sons

A FOLKTALE FROM INDIA
BY ASMA SAYED

Once upon a time, in a little village named Munjka in the Gujarat province in India, there was an old farmer. The farmer had four sons who helped him with the farm work. The farmer was getting very old. He was worried that his sons might not work together after his death, and that if they failed to plough the land and grow a decent crop they might lose their land to the greedy moneylenders. It would be very important that everybody divided the tasks and worked together.

One day, the farmer called all his sons. He asked them to go and each bring a branch from a tree. The sons wondered what their father was up to. They all headed out, and each came back with a branch in his hands.

Now, the farmer asked each of his sons to break his own branch; he said to his first son, *"Dikra,* my son, I want you to break that branch into two."

The son was quite amused, and said, *"Bapuji,* father, I don't understand why you want me to do this, but since you say so, here ..." and he folded the branch in the middle and it broke into two pieces. Then, the farmer asked his other three sons to do the same with the branches that they were holding. They all broke them, one by one.

Then, the father requested his sons to go out again, and bring another branch from a tree. The sons didn't understand why their father was asking them to do this meaningless task, but they knew they were supposed to respect their elders and do what they were asked to do. They were sure their father must surely have some plan. So again they headed out, and each came back with a branch in his hand. The youngest son was very excited,

"Bapuji, bapuji, I know what we have to do; you want us to break these branches into two, right?"

The father said, "No, this time I want you to put all of your branches together and tie the bundle with a string."

So the oldest brother collected all the four branches, the second son went and got a string, the third one tied the string around the branches, and the fourth one then showed it to their father.

The father then spoke to the youngest son, "Now, please break these branches."

The youngest son tried, but he couldn't break the branches; he then asked his older brother to try, but even he couldn't. All four brothers took turns trying to break the branches, but none of them succeeded. The father explained, "See, my sons, if you put the branches together, their strength increases, and nobody can break them. United we stand, and divided we fall. When I die, please stay together and work with each other, and no one will ever be able to separate you."

The sons now perceived what their father had done—he had taught them one of the most valuable lessons of life. They promised their father that they would never forget the advice he had given them.

AUTHOR'S NOTE

The origins of this story probably go back to *Panchtantra*—the oldest collection of tales from India. As I grew up in the Gujarat province in India, I heard this story many times—from family members as well as from school teachers; it is one of the most popular stories that circulates in India in various forms. Although rooted in the rural setting of farming communities in India, the story has a universal moral of staying together in good and bad times. Children must learn the values of team spirit and working together, and the metaphor of a branch explains this message well.

The Storyteller

A Canadian
Multicultural Folktale
by Roxanne Felix

A long time ago—when the earth was still young, the seas were still warm and people did not yet roam the earth—the Great Mother, maker of all, lived close to those whom she created. She lived so close, that she spoke with them every day, hearing all of their concerns, complaints, hopes, and wishes. But once a year, she grew tired of listening to them. She would fall into a great deep sleep, and the sun would rest with her so that everyone had to live for a short time under a deep blanket of cold and ice. When it came time for the Great Mother to take her rest, the creatures and elements would protest and grumble, for they did not like it when she left. And every year the protests and the grumbling grew louder and longer, until finally the Great Mother got angry and decided they needed a lesson.

"Every year," she said, "I am with you from the first unfolding of the blossoms until the leaves change their colours and fall to the earth. And still, that is not enough? I will do this no more. See how you live without me." And with those words she retreated high into the heavens, higher than she had ever gone before. The Great Mother's creatures were astonished and distressed. What would they do without the Great Mother?

Finally, after many discussions and arguments, the grizzly bear bounded in front of all the other creatures and elements. "I will take the Great Mother's place," he announced with a growl. The others considered it and nodded their heads quickly in agreement. The grizzly bear would do well. He was frightening and strong and bold. He could maintain order. But the Great Mother, who secretly watched her children from high above, just smiled. The grizzly bear did very well. He strutted about and told the sun when he should set, commanded the wolves to stop fighting over their territories and ordered the porcupine not to chew too much wood.

Oh yes, the grizzly bear did very well! But then the creatures and elements got tired of his bullying ways. And when the grizzly bear wasn't looking, the creatures took more food than they needed, the stars did not twinkle as brightly as they were supposed to and the sea did not care if his waves were too strong. The bear began to grow weary, for he could not be everywhere at once. Finally, he shouted, "Enough! The Great Mother was right. This is too much to do!" With a sigh, he announced he was no longer in charge.

Now, everyone had mixed feelings about the bear's announcement. They were relieved to be rid of all the grizzly bear's rules, but they also knew they still needed order. Amidst all the discussions and arguments about what to do next, the fox spoke up. She darted in front of the others, her red fur gleaming in the sun. "I will take the Great Mother's place," she murmured. Everyone considered this announcement and nodded their heads slowly in agreement. The fox was clever and shrewd and swift. She could maintain order. But, the Great Mother just smiled again from her place high in the skies.

The fox did very well. She glided about and watched others' activities silently. When the moon rose too late, the fox tricked her into coming earlier. When the lynx hunted too much, the fox bribed him into eating only his fill by promising more food next year. And when the skunk took too many leaves for her den, the fox spoke badly of her to all the others until the skunk behaved.

Oh yes, the fox did very well! But then the creatures and elements grew resentful of the fox's tricky ways. And when the fox wasn't looking, the creatures gathered more branches for their homes than they really needed, the raindrops did not fall as lightly as they should have and the wind thought it didn't matter if she blew too hard. The fox began to get impatient, for she could not be everywhere at once, until she sullenly announced, "No more! The Great Mother was right. This world is too much to handle!" With a flick of her tail, she announced she was no longer in charge.

Now the creatures really began to worry. For if the grizzly bear and the fox could not maintain order, who could? A silence fell among them. Then, without warning, the chickadee fluttered in front of the other creatures, the feathers on her black cap rustling in the breeze and her white cheeks rosy with embarrassment. "I will take the Great Mother's place," she chirped.

The creatures broke into laughter.

"You?" chortled the crane. "All you do is eat bugs!" Everyone continued to snicker (except for the insects, of course, who felt insulted). But no one else volunteered, so the creatures shrugged and let the chickadee try. The Great Mother, however, became serious, for she was surprised at the chickadee's words.

The chickadee did not do so well. All she did was flit about and visit. Oh, the sun enjoyed her company well enough, but noted that the chickadee did not really pay attention to when he rose and set. The porcupine appreciated the little bird's questions about her home, but admitted the chickadee did nothing to provide order. The swan delighted in sharing the meaning of his songs, but confessed the chickadee did not do much except listen.

Then, just when everyone began to wonder when the chickadee would do something—anything—the chickadee summoned them all to a meeting. They were certain she would also announce that she would no longer be in charge (though they thought she hadn't really been in charge anyway). But, instead, she asked them to be silent.

Then she began to tell a story, a tale about the falcon travelling on the winds to find food for his family who had nested in the high cliffs. And the wind remembered the Great Mother telling her that many birds of the sky always depended on the wind's currents to fly far and wide.

The next night, the chickadee invited them back and recounted how the marten had lived through the winter by using the squirrels' tunnels to find food. And the squirrels remembered the Great Mother describing how many forest animals always relied on squirrels' burrows to survive under the thick snowfalls.

The next night, the chickadee told of the dangerous journeys of the caribou across the windy plains and pointed out which constellations of stars they used to find their way. And the stars remembered the Great Mother explaining how the prairie creatures trusted in the stars' brilliant patterns of light to be guided home.

Night by night, the chickadee told a different story about each of the creatures and elements, and all of them gathered to hear every one. And, slowly, ever so slowly, without any orders or tricks from the chickadee, the Great Mother's children began to create order among themselves. The Great Mother looked down and was pleased, for she had forgotten that the chickadee could tell stories and how important stories were. And she decided to stay in her place in the heavens, watching the creatures and elements grow to live in harmony.

But, the Great Mother knew that for peace to last she needed to reserve a special place in her realm for the chickadee and her stories. So, to this day, the chickadee continues to chatter in the winds, never stopping her storytelling throughout the four seasons.

Author's Note

The Storyteller is a story filled with Canadian spirit. I was inspired to write this fable based on my experiences working with immigrants and refugees in Edmonton, Alberta. In a settlement agency, one of the first things you learn is that the story of an individual or family is important. Sometimes, in Canada, we ask about a person's statistics or facts, but we forget to take the time to ask about a person's journey. But by sharing stories, we learn not only how much we have in common, but how much we depend upon each other, as a community. I hoped that this fable would reflect how a strong community can be built, if we listen to one another, value each other's history and recognize our interdependence.

Abrahams, Roger D., comp. *African Folktales.*
New York: Pantheon, 1983.

Afanasev, Alexander, comp. *Russian Fairy Tales.*
Trans. Norbert Guterman. New York: Pantheon, 1945.

Asbjørnsen, Peter, and Jorgen Moe, comps.
Popular Tales from the Norse. Trans. Sir George Webbe Dasent.
New York: D. Appleton, 1859.

Briggs, Katherine M., and Ruth L. Tongue.
Folktales of England. Chicago: U of Chicago P, 1965.

Bushnaq, Inea, comp. *Arab Folktales.* New York: Pantheon, 1986.

Calvino, Italo, comp. *Italian Folktales.*
Trans. George Martin. New York: Pantheon, 1980.

Chase, Richard, comp. *American Folk Tales and Songs.*
New York: Signet, 1956.

Crossley-Holland, Kevin, comp. *Folktales of the British Isles.*
New York: Pantheon, 1988.

Dawkins, R.M., comp. *Modern Greek Folktales.*
Oxford: Clarendon, 1953.

Delarue, Paul, comp. *Borzoi Book of French Folk Tales.*
Trans. Austin E. Fife. New York: Knopf, 1956.

Eberhard, Wolfram, comp. *Folktales of China.*
Chicago: U of Chicago P, 1975.

Jacobs, Joseph, comp. *Celtic Fairy Tales.* London: D. Nutt, 1892.

Noy, Dov, comp. *Folktales of Israel.*
Trans. Gene Baharav. Chicago: U of Chicago P, 1963.

Pourrat, Henri, comp. *French Folktales.*
Trans. Royall Tyler. New York: Pantheon, 1989.

Ramanujan, A.K., comp. *Folktales from India.*
New York: Random House, 1991.

Ranke, Kurt, comp. *Folktales of Germany.*
Trans. Lotte Baumann. Chicago: U of Chicago P, 1966.

Rugoff, Milton A., comp. *A Harvest of World Folk Tales.*
New York: Viking, 1949.

Simpson, Jacqueline, comp. *Icelandic Folktales and Legends.*
Berkeley: U of California P, 1972.

Thompson, Stith, comp. *Tales of the North American Indians.*
Bloomington: Indiana UP, 1929.

Weinrich, Beatrice Silverman, comp. *Yiddish Folktales.*
New York: Pantheon, 1988.

Yolen, Jane. *Favorite Folktales from Around the World.*
New York: Pantheon, 1986.

Zipes, Jack. *Spells of Enchantment: The Wondrous Fairy Tales of
Western Culture.* New York: Viking, 1991.

CONTRIBUTING AUTHORS

Antoinette Botsford

Antoinette is a storyteller with Canadian grandparents of rural French-Canadian and Métis (believed to be primarily Ojibwe) origin. Her grandparents emigrated to the Peace River country of Alberta early in the last century, where they raised cattle, bees and quite a few children. They later homesteaded in Washington state, maintaining dual citizenship. Antoinette was born in Spokane, Washington and now lives on Orcas Island. She frequently tells stories in Canada and enjoys visiting her Canadian brother and sister-in-law, who have a tree farm near Edmonton.

Nataliya Bukhanova and **Dave Schultz**

Nataliya Bukhanova is a recent immigrant from Russia, born and raised in Ekaterinburg, near the Ural Mountains of Central Russia. In Russia she held a Ph.D. and worked as an Associate Professor of Pharmacology, and was a working artist and graphic designer. Since arriving in Canada in 2007 to be with her husband, David, she has concentrated on her artwork, participating in several shows in Edmonton. She is currently re-entering the academic community, working as a research assistant in the Pharmacology department at the University of Alberta.

David Schultz is Canadian-born and was raised in Saskatchewan. David has been in the Canadian Forces since 1991, and through them has travelled extensively.

Ed Butts

Ed is an author of several published books including *SOS: Stories of Survival, She Dared, X Doesn't Mark the Spot* and *Line of Fire: Heroism, Tragedy, and Canada's Police.* He has also written a humourous book about English grammar called *Idioms For Aliens,* and has written lyrics for educational songs for children. He taught school in the Dominican Republic for eight years. He now lives in Guelph with his daughter and four-year-old grandson.

Roxanne Felix

Roxanne has only three wishes: to spend her summers in Prince Edward Island, to deliver the perfect Muay-Thai roundhouse kick and to lengthen the nights—for that's when she writes. As a result of her night owl habits, she has published several short stories and recently collaborated on an anthology of novellas entitled *Women of the Apocalypse,* a winner of the Aurora award, which recognizes exceptional Canadian written work in Science Fiction and Fantasy. Drop by her website at www.roxannefelix.com.

Pearl-Ann Gooding

Pearl-Ann has been a professional storyteller since 1993, working for and on behalf of Storytellers of Canada/Conteurs du Canada and TALES (The Alberta League Encouraging Storytelling), as well as freelancing. Family, faerie, folk and ghost stories are her specialty. She has several storytelling CDs of her work, as well as inclusions in both written and oral anthologies.

Mary Hays and **Louis Soop**

Mary Hays, from Olds, Alberta, is a full-time storyteller who enjoys telling folktales and stories of Alberta history, including those of the Blackfoot people. Louis Soop has mentored Mary in the telling of the stories of his people. They have collaborated on various storytelling projects.

Louis Soop, of the Blood Nation, is a cultural consultant and a teacher of Blackfoot Studies and Language. He has a keen interest in preserving the artifacts and stories of his Blood elders and members of the Horn Society. He delights in storytelling, traditional dancing and drumming as a way to share the rich culture of the people of the Blood-Kainai Nation with children and people of all ages around the world.

Maria Teresa Olszewska Hopkins

Maria was born in Gdańsk, Poland, in a family of six children whom she, as oldest sibling, had to entertain by storytelling, as her mother did for her. During volunteer work for the World Esperanto Congress held in Warsaw in 1987, Maria met Paul, a Canadian, whom she married, and then they came to Canada with daughter Agnieszka. They lived first in Paul's hometown of Victoria, British Columbia for 10 years, and then in St. Catharines, Ontario for another four years, before moving to Calgary, Alberta in 2005. Maria has had a rich career as a food technologist, health care worker and child care worker, but for the past 15 years she has increasingly dedicated her life to the arts, and is now a full-time storyteller and artist.

Kathy Jessup

Kathy is a storyteller and writer based in Edmonton, Alberta. For nearly 20 years she has performed her original stories and favourite folktales in schools and libraries, and at concerts and festivals across Canada. Being of Irish descent, Kathy has a special fondness for stories from the 'Emerald Isle.' Drop by her website at www.kathyjessup.com

Melissa Morelli Lacroix

Melissa is a writer, writing facilitator and speaker who lives and works in Edmonton, Alberta. Language, culture and family are commonly explored in her work. Her writing has been produced on CBC Radio and on stage at the University of Alberta, and published in Canadian, American and British publications, such as *Ars Medica, In the Red, The Dawntreader, Legacy, Other Voices,* and *Family Pictures: Poems and Photographs Celebrating Our Loved Ones.*

Danielle Lamb

Danielle is in her second year of the Comparative Literature Doctoral Program at the University of Alberta. In 2003, she had the opportunity to live and study in Guadalajara. One of the highlights of her time in Mexico was teaching at her host mother's Kinder (playschool) where she had the opportunity to share children's stories from her childhood in Canada, and to learn new stories from the children she taught.

Shoshana Litman

Shoshana became Canada's first ordained Maggidah, a traditional Jewish storyteller, speaker, and teacher, in May 2008. She is a featured storyteller at Tall Tales Books in Victoria, an administrator for The Mussar Institute of Vancouver, and a regular contributor to the Times Colonist newspaper's blog, *Spiritually Speaking.* Also known as Suzanne Kort Litman, she is a published author with a degree in environmental science. Shoshana and her husband, Todd Litman, have raised two fine sons who love to learn.

Jennifer Maruno

After 35 years in education, Jennifer retired to write for children. Magazines in Canada, Britain and the United States have published several of her stories. Napoleon Publishing launched her first novel, *When the Cherry Blossoms Fell,* a historical fiction for 8- to 12-year-olds, in 2009. It is a finalist for the 2011 Hackmatack Children's Choice Book Award. *Warbird,* her latest historical adventure, appeared in November, 2010. Jennifer is a member of the Canadian Society of Children's Authors, Illustrators and Performers (CANSCAIP), and the Society of Children's Book Writers and Illustrators (SCBWI). She lives in Burlington, Ontario, home to the Carolinian Forest.

Catherine Melnyk

Catherine is a second year Master of Arts student in Comparative Literature with a focus in Disability Studies at the University of Alberta. Raised on an acreage just outside of Edmonton, Catherine has always imagined that the fairy tales she grew up hearing could have occurred in her own backyard.

Faye Mogensen

Faye Mogensen, M.Ed., lives on Vancouver Island with her husband, three children, one cat and about 15 chickens. She tends a large organic garden but gets away to the wilderness whenever she can. She's proud of her adventurous family, her Scandinavian heritage, her membership in the Victoria Storytellers' Guild and her Masters of Education—with a focus on storytelling as a tool for environmental education. Faye's speciality is weaving folklore, personal story, history and science into tales of mystery, humour and passion; these are the stories she often shares at the First Unitarian Church of Victoria, where she now works as an educator.

Jurate Motiejunaite

Jurate was born in Lithuania, a small Eastern European country near the Baltic Sea. She has finished her Ph.D. studies in Comparative Literature at the University of Alberta, and is currently teaching Comparative Literature and Writing courses at Grant MacEwan University and the University of Alberta.

Marghalara Rashid

Marghalara is originally from Afghanistan; she moved to India, where she lived for 10 years. She came to Canada to pursue her higher education, where she finished her B.A., and is currently working on her master's degree at the University of Alberta.

Estelle Salata

As she was growing up, award-winning author Estelle Salata always loved animal stories best. She read *Watership Down* several times as an adult; it's not surprising that she went on to write a bestselling series featuring talking mice and rats pitted against each other in sports. *Mice at Centre Ice* was turned into a popular animated film (see www.estellesalata.ca). Estelle's favourite folktale features a talking spider and a turtle.

Dalbir Sehmby

Dalbir received his doctorate in Comparative Literature and Film/Media Studies from the University of Alberta. He has won the U of A Frank Beukert playwriting award and a U of A teaching award. Internationally, he has served as a Head of Curriculum at Mažas Pasaulis School of Language and Communication (in Kaunas, Lithuania), and as an educator and Communications Consultant for the International Debate Education Association (IDEA). Currently, he teaches English at the University of Alberta's Campus Saint Jean in Edmonton.

Nathalie Vachon

Nathalie is a writer, performer, storyteller and painter living in the Toronto Beaches. She lived in Japan for a year and a half, and draws from her experiences there in many of the stories and paintings she creates. You can see more of her work at www.nathalievachon.com.

Henry Victor

Dr. Henry Victor, former Senior Lecturer in Comparative Religion in the Eastern University, Sri Lanka, has been a sessional instructor in the Religious Studies program at the University of Alberta since 2001. He is also a widely-published poet, who tells stories through his poetry. At present, he is an accredited interpreter/translator for the Canadian government in English/Tamil languages.

Phyllis Walker

Phyllis is a retired school teacher who has turned her passion for storytelling into a vehicle for empowering children. Visits to perform in libraries and various schools have allowed her to see just how pleased children are to hear stories. Teaching allowed her to have her multicultural class share stories from different cultures in the classroom, and has given her the opportunity to help to make the world a better place.

Xie Wenjuan

Xie is a second year Ph.D. student in Comparative Literature at the University of Alberta. She loves folktales and dreams of one day becoming a great storyteller like her grandma. She is currently researching fantasy heroines in Chinese ghost stories, and is determined to make folklore study her life career.

Latika Srivastava

Latika Srivastava has an LL.M., and has taught as a Professor of Law at the University of Delhi, India. She has written on a variety of topics including criminal and civil justice systems in Canada, personal and religious laws that govern marriages and divorces in different faith communities, misuse of international arranged marriages as marriages of convenience or marriages for immigration purposes, and cultural malpractices that lead to domestic violence in South-Asian communities. Latika is one of the co-authors of the book *International Arranged Marriages.* She is an activist in the areas of child labour legislations and public interest litigations.

Resource Development Services, Edmonton Public Schools

Resource Development Services (RDS) develops curriculum-aligned resources to support the work of teaching and learning that occurs in K–12 schools across Canada. Developed by teachers, RDS resources are created in response to the valuable input received from school staff and support the emerging and diverse needs of today's classrooms. Some of RDS's 75+ print and online resources focus on core curriculum, many offer supplementary support, and a number are translated into a range of languages. For more information, visit rds.epsb.net.

The RDS project team for *World on a Maple Leaf: A Treasury of Canadian Multicultural Folktales* consists of:

Dana Antayā-Moore, Supervisor
Flavio Rojas, Illustrator
Helen Adhikari, Graphic Designer
Karen Haukedal, Editor

Special thanks to Deborah Lawson of Word Circus, Inc. for final edits.

Advisory Committee Members

Dr. Nayanika Kumar—*see page 102*

Catherine Ripley

Catherine Ripley, an author of many books for young children, is currently working on her 20th book. She has also enjoyed a successful editorial career with publications such as *Cricket, Chickadee, Global Biodiversity* and *The Riverbend Ragg-Times*. Between 2000 and 2007, she was an instructor with the Institute of Children's Literature. Graduates of Trent University, Catherine and her husband have been married for 29 years, and have three adult children. Catherine is also entering her second term as an Edmonton Public Schools Trustee. She is committed to ensuring community members have a voice in shaping future directions for Edmonton Public Schools. Catherine believes in a warm welcome for all students and families, and is eager to put public education and its value into the hearts and minds of the entire community.

Dr. Asma Sayed—*see page 102*

Dr. Carol Suddards

Carol Suddards was born in Edmonton, and attended Edmonton Public Schools, the University of Alberta (B.Ed., 1973) and the University of Calgary (M.A., 1997; Ph.D., 2004). Her research interests are in community participation and collaboration, and educational leadership. Throughout her 32-year career in education, she worked toward equal educational outcomes for all students, and the promotion of lifelong learning among students, teachers, parents and community members of all ages. Since leaving public education, she has worked as a consultant to educational and other organizations, providing strategic support to senior management. She is a trustee of the Edmonton Public Library Board, a member of Toastmasters International, an active member of her professional community, a writer and workshop presenter. Carol enjoys travelling, hiking, cross-country skiing, music and pilates. She is an avid reader and collector of books.

Dr. Asma Sayed

Asma Sayed holds an M.A. in English, and a Ph.D. in Comparative Literature from the University of Alberta; she teaches courses in Comparative Literature, English, Women's Studies and Communication Studies at the University of Alberta, Grant MacEwan University and Athabasca University. Asma specializes in Canadian ethnic minority writing, and her research focuses on women's studies, post-colonial literature and cultural studies. Asma has published in her areas of interest and research. She has translated folktales from Gujarati, and taught courses on fairy tales and folktales. A mother of three children, Asma has called Edmonton 'home' since she migrated to Canada in 1998.

I would like to thank United Cultures of Canada Association and Nayanika Kumar for giving me an opportunity to be a part of this exciting project; working on this book has been a great experience. I am grateful to Dr. Irene Sywenky for introducing me to the wonderful world of folktales and fairy tales. Thanks are also due to Dr. Jonathan Hart, who has been a source of inspiration. I express my appreciation to all the authors who have contributed their stories; this project would not have materialized without support and interest of all the contributors.

Dr. Nayanika Kumar

Nayanika Kumar has her M.A. and Ph.D. in English Literature, and Bachelor degrees in Arts and Teaching. Since 1998, she has been engaged in writing and research, and a wide range of settlement initiatives aimed at promoting integrated and vibrant communities. She is one of the co-authors of *International Arranged Marriages,* a book that discusses immigration and legal issues associated with international arranged marriages in Canada. Nayanika was honoured with the Queen's Golden Jubilee Medal in 2002 in recognition of her community work. She lives in Edmonton with her husband and two children.

There is an old saying in Sanskrit, 'Vasudhaiva Kutumbakam,' which means that this whole world is but one single family. This adage never seemed more meaningful to me than it does now, in the context of multicultural Canada. While working on this project, it felt as if the entire project team, including its authors, reviewers, advisory members, consultants, editors, publisher and illustrator, was joined together by a common vision of Canada, a global village that is home to hundreds of nationalities of the world. I express my gratitude to all the authors and reviewers. I would like to especially thank Nicholas Amayew and Catherine Ripley, who helped to explore the project idea and also provided consistent support and guidance for its successful completion. Thank you, Carol Suddards and Asma Sayed, for sharing freely your valuable insights and expertise. Thank you to the publishing team: Dana Antayā-Moore, Flavio Rojas, Helen Adhikari, and Karen Haukedal, for completing with perfection what I had very humbly started.